Published by Ad Hoc Fiction.
www.AdHocFiction.com

Purchasing Information:
Paperback available from www.AdHocFiction.com

E-book available from all usual outlets.
Printed in the United Kingdom.
First Printing 2021.

ISBN paperback 978-1-912095-31-5
ISBN e-Book 978-1-912095-30-8

The Bath Short Story Award Anthology 2021

Compiled by

Jude Higgins, Jane Riekemann and Alison Woodhouse

AdHoc Fiction

Introduction

Welcome to our eighth print anthology, published again by the award-winning Ad Hoc Fiction; the first, in 2013, was produced as an ebook in collaboration with *Good Housekeeping* magazine. Each anthology has comprised a diverse and eclectic selection of stories and 2021 is no exception. This year we received 1,210 stories from around the globe, and for the duration of the award the world has been gripped by the Covid-19 pandemic, where lockdowns and daily graphs of grim statistics have become the norm. So, no surprise then that, although Covid hasn't featured overtly in the stories we received, themes of despair, grief, loss and dystopian elements are present in much of the writing, with moments of beauty emerging through the bleakness.

Judging our shortlist was Norah Perkins from Curtis Brown and we thank her for her hard work and the thoughtful and incisive comments she made on the winning stories. These are her overall observations:

'*It was a very great pleasure and an honour to judge the 2021 Bath Short Story Award. I work primarily with writers who are no longer alive but whose work lives on and is treasured by generations of readers. And so for me especially it is always exciting to have the opportunity to read new voices, and to imagine the ways that these writers will continue to interpret their world, and to bring their stories to us lucky readers in the years to come.*

In a year when so many have suffered, when so many social and economic injustices have been brought – yet again – into harsh relief, I feel ever more keenly that stories have the capacity to help us listen to each other, to draw us closer together, to help us process the complex world we all share, and ultimately to bring us a sense of connection and hope. The stories in this year's shortlist were, every one of them, extraordinary, and it was inevitably a difficult task to choose a winner. All the stories spoke eloquently – often in the voices of children and of those who have in some way been marginalised – of memory, of poverty, of mental health, of identity, and of the ways that love and anger intersect. And so many of them spoke of loss, in so many different forms, and the way that loss takes shape in our lives. And yet there was great beauty and humour and passion, too – the flip side of our human coin. The winners of this year's Award all demonstrate radical compassion, diverse perspectives, and truly extraordinary voices – I can't wait to read what they write next.'

Many congratulations to our winners: First Prize, 'In Bed With My Sister' by K. Lockwood Jefford from the UK (incidentally another of her stories is in our first anthology); Second Prize, 'Davey, Plastic Jesus and the Holy Spirit' by Stephanie Carty from the UK; Third Prize, 'Important Letters' by Kristen Loesch from the USA. Highly commended were Linda Wang for 'Ma's Favourite' and Lynda Mason for 'The Great Pretender', both from the UK. Lynda also won The Acorn Award, set up by us a few years ago to champion unpublished writers. Our Local Prize, donated by Mr B's Emporium of Books, was won by Bristol writer Ruth Bateson for 'The Pheasant'.

We hope you enjoy this collection, and if you're inspired to write, our next award will open in November 2021 and end in April 2022. Do subscribe for email notifications and to read news and interviews from all our winners, past and present. All details can be found on our website bathshortstoryaward.org. You can also follow us on Twitter @BathStoryAward.

Contents

K. Lockwood Jefford

In Bed With My Sister

'Why are you doing this?'

My sister's voice barely a breath, her face looming – flat and wide as a dinnerplate – and glowing with greenish light in the grainy not-quite-darkness of the room. The spare room. (She won't sleep in her own room.) Curtains made by our mother. Grey-green, silk, rough to the touch like five o'clock shadow.

A siren streets away. Always a siren in the city. The cat scratches the door.

It feels as if time is paused, poised to unfurl a thin night strung out on watered-down sleep.

'Your hand is too close.' Her whispered words brush my ear, hang in the scrawny air.

I am very conscious of my body, of its reach, its parts. I lie flat on my back. Like they tell me to. The physios, chiros, osteos. Every kind of expert I've seen. Slippy discs, they say. Off-kilter pelvis. Knotted muscles, frayed tendons. Torsion, scoliosis, kyphosis. Don't cross your legs or sleep on your front. Do stretches, lunges, planks, bridges. Downward-facing dog.

Sometimes I walk like an old woman. In bed with my sister, I feel like a child. A monster child, my head too big. All our heads too big. Big babies we were, our mother says, especially our heads.

Three of us. Sisters. Me the oldest, her the youngest. One in the middle.

My sister's silent but I sense she's still awake. Brittle, she's been lately. Terse on the phone. And talking, talking, talking. Rapid, forceful words shooting out like boxers' fists. Thrusting, punching my ears. Pummelling inside my head. Exhausting, it's been. I wanted to reach down the line to press one hand over her mouth – my palm moistening from her hot, shallow breath – while my other tried to push a word in sideways like a coin in a slot-machine.

Last week, she called me when I was on a train.

'What's that noise?' she said.

'It's the automatic doors beeping,' I said.

'It sounds like a police siren,' she'd said. A hushed voice. 'It makes me think you're not the right person to talk to.'

Childhood. She's been talking a lot about childhood. The smell of TCP. Taste of malt in our mouths at bedtime. A shadow. Legs slipping on cold nylon sheets. A pair of balled-up knickers covered in bedroom fluff. Her childhood, her memories. Shadows lurking in the corners of her mind blurring into mine.

Little girls playing in the dark. Three of us squashed in one bed. A magic carpet, a sports car, Concorde. Our mother's clomp on the stairs. Bare feet running on floorboards. Bedroom door banged open. Light snapped on. Sheets whipped back. Red handprints burning our legs.

Doctors and Nurses in our vests and knickers. I'd lay my sisters down and examine them. Chests and tummies and down there. We rubbed our privates faster faster and screamed with brazen delight.

A pair of balled-up knickers covered in bedroom fluff.

Your hand is too close.

It's fingers that do the probing, poking, pulling and twiddling.

Whose? Whose?

I lie on my back, still as a corpse, hands by my sides, palms up.

She's taken down the pictures in her room and placed them on the floor facing the wall as if in disgrace. Earlier, she lifted one by its string-slung back to show me. Classic kitsch Woolworth's print. 1960s. It used to hang in our nana's house. A portrait of a woman with greeny-blue skin, lips too red, dress too gold for us to understand. We called her the Green Lady.

'She gives me the creeps,' my sister said. 'I can't sleep with her watching.'

Nana's house was where we'd spend school holidays. Out from under our mother's feet. Nana let us play in the woods. Tarzan on a rope swing. Secret dens in dappled enclaves. Picnics. Cream crackers and Dairylea triangles.

'Whoever said you had a God-given right to happiness?'

Our mother shouting. Divorce papers on the bedside table. Harveys Bristol Cream hidden behind her dresses in the wardrobe. Dresses that didn't fit after three kids. And where would she wear them anyway?

My sister's memories merging with mine. Our mother banging on the bathroom door. The only door in the house that locked. Sitting on the lid of the toilet where she flushed our contraceptive pills.

'I missed you when you left.'

I was the buffer between us and our mother. Shouting back. Fighting at the top of the stairs. Falling. Landing on my back.

I couldn't wait to leave and go to medical school. The middle one met a man and moved to Mississippi where she loves living close to hurricane escape routes. The youngest stayed the longest.

One time I came home and found a notebook next to her bed. I didn't know it was her diary until I started reading. Then I couldn't stop because it was about me.

She says she'll be home this weekend. She always says that then she never comes.

'I missed you when you left.'

My sister's words tugging at a loose thread. Could unravel me.

And if I was sleeping in her bed back then, where was she? Was it one of the times she ran away?

They always brought her back.

Troubled she was back then. The troubled one. I was the brainy one. The middle one was the middle one.

Counselling. My sister's been talking about counselling. Saw two counsellors in three days.

The first one let her sit on the floor, and they 'clicked'. But she lives the other side of the city.

'Taxi fares on top of the fees wouldn't be feasible,' my sister said. 'Fee. Sible. Siblings.'

'What?' I said.

'Sibs. Fibs.'

She called me after seeing the second counsellor who was around the corner, her voice small and hollow, as if she was inside my phone. A Thumbelina sister muffled in my hand.

'I think I should call the police,' she said

'The police?' I said.

'I've done something terrible.'

A gun went off inside me, bounced along my bones, echoed in my head.

'I don't think you're well,' I said.

'Should I call the doctor?'

'Where are you?'

'I'm in the *Co-op*. Some nice people brought me in here.'

One of the nice people came on the phone to say my sister had been confused and lost on the street. Couldn't find her way home.

That was Friday.

Friday my sister waited seven hours in A&E to see a nurse another nurse and a doctor before she was discharged to the care of the mental health crisis team.

Friday I called our mother.

'I've bought the tickets now. It's all planned. What could I do anyway?' she said.

Be a mother, I didn't say.

Saturday our mother boarded a Virgin plane to Dallas for a connecting flight to Biloxi-Gulfport, Mississippi.

Saturday I caught a train to see my sister, racing west under a sky bruised and bloated with an impending storm.

My sister at the door. Her skin dull, her green eyes grey, narrowed, suspicious.

'Did you see the police car?' she said.

'Where?' I said.

'Around the corner. They know.'

She sat down, stood up. She raised her arms, dropped them.

'People fear the truth of what they see when they pass me in the street. It's why they look away.'

She sat down, stood up, sat down again. A flash of sheet lightning illuminated her tormented form. A scene in a noir film.

'Surveillance,' she said. 'They are coming for me.'

I looked at the box of pills from the hospital. Low-dose diazepam. I called the number for the crisis team and asked if they could prescribe something stronger. They said the psychiatrist was busy. I said my sister was persecuted by her thoughts. They said the psychiatrist was at another site. I said my sister was suffering. They said it would be difficult to … it would be better if…

They said she could see someone tomorrow.

I doubled the dose.

'Are you awake?'

My sister raises herself on a single pointy elbow. I sense it in the listing of the mattress. I picture her shoulder blades, bony butterfly wings cutting through her skin, the bumps of her spine beneath her skimpy layer of flesh. In two pregnancies she swelled and bloomed. Two boys. Only one left.

'Why has it taken me this long to face what I've done? It's too little, too late. I put my children at risk.'

Ten years ago, her younger son was killed outside his school when another parent's SUV mounted the pavement. Tonight, she asks if he's really dead.

'Yes,' I say.

She doesn't believe me, says he's alive and living with people who can look after him properly. Says the middle sister isn't really in Mississippi but living somewhere else in secret. Says I'm an actor impersonating her sister. The real people have to protect themselves from her.

'I will die in prison alone for what I did.'

I want to reach out, hold her. But touching has gone bad.

Your hand is too close.

I ball up my fists and squeeze.

My mind is slipping, my thoughts softening, dissolving into my sister's and I can't keep track and

I'm in Nana's house.

The summer she had lodgers. Men in oily dungarees, quick change, fresh shirt, smelling of pine soap. Shaving brushes in the bathroom. Razors, under-arm deodorant, jars of gel for slicked-back Saturday nights. Aftershave. Whiff of leather and limes. Men's hands tickling, lifting. Piggy backs, shoulder rides, tall, tall, ducking under the fake chandelier in the hall. Men's fingerprints on our legs. Men's hands with short nails, not our mother's ripping ones.

Nana kept her hands to herself, no smacks. No cuddles either.

Your hand is too close.

Whose? Whose?

The nice lodger, Len. The other one, Steve, staring eyes and pinchy-proddy hands. No, my sisters say. Steve was the nice one. Our mother says Nana talked about getting lodgers, but never did.

I wake I don't know how much later, and my sister's gone. I leap up. As I fly down the stairs the cat reaches through the banister railings and scratches my cheek.

My sister is sat at the kitchen table rolling a cigarette.

'I'm trying to give up,' she says.

'It's not the time,' I say.

'I should give myself up.'

She says this loudly. For a hidden eavesdropper. A spy.

In the yellowy early daylight, I see her fingernails are filthy and cracked, the cuticles ragged. Large hands for such a small person. Sculptor's hands. Usually caked in clay. Across the hall her studio door is bolted and padlocked.

'I've been fooling everyone I'm creative when I've been destructive all along. Why has it taken me so long to see?'

The cat jumps onto the table. My cheek throbs. I touch the sandpapery graze left by its claw.

'He knows,' she says. 'I can tell by the sidelong looks he's giving me. He's not my real cat. The police have trained him to monitor me.'

'Let's go back to bed,' I say. 'In the morning Nick from the crisis team is coming to take us to see the psychiatrist.'

'Nick?' she says. 'Hah! He's coming to nick me. Trick me. Prick me to see if I'm real.'

In the morning the psychiatrist will be even smaller than my sister. Doll-sized. Perfectly proportioned in a well-cut woollen trouser suit. Italian. She must feel the cold. She will walk briskly on click-clack heels, clutching my sister's slim file and swinging a curtain of shiny black hair behind her. We will follow her along long draughty corridors, bare windows and strip-lighting, turning corner after corner after corner to a cold room where we'll sit on a plastic sofa facing the psychiatrist sitting on her hair.

And my sister will be zipped up. Dry lips schtum. And I'll steer her to tell the psychiatrist what she's told me. And my sister will start talking and we'll both cry.

And the psychiatrist will say my sister is articulate.

'Like a lorry,' my sister will say.

The psychiatrist will write a prescription for medication that she says will make my sister better, but also fat.

But that's in the morning.

Tonight, in bed with my sister, I picture our mother in the sky in her favourite seat where she doesn't have to talk to anyone. And I remember the time I told her I wasn't going to have any children.

And she said, 'No, I didn't think you would. I suppose you had enough looking after your sisters.'

I don't know if that's it.

Or if not having kids is a way of showing my mother what I think of her.

'Why are you doing this?'

My sister reaches across the bed and grasps my hand in her scissors-paper-stone hand.

And I hold her hand back.

Like a sister. Or a mother.

I know there's a difference. I don't know what it is.

It feels the same.

K. Lockwood Jefford is from Cardiff, where she grew up obsessed with books and cartwheels. She worked in NHS and student mental health services – alongside a stint writing and performing stand-up comedy – before completing an MA in creative writing, Birkbeck. Her story 'Picasso's Face' won the 2020 VS Pritchett Prize. She's been shortlisted for Bath and Rhys Davies awards in 2021. Her work appears in *MIR Online* and anthologies including Bristol (2017), Sunderland-Waterstones (first prize 2019), Brick Lane Bookshop (third prize 2020) and is forthcoming in Fish Publishing (2021) and 100 Voices (Unbound). She's working on a collection of stories.

First Prize
Comments from judge Norah Perkins

Heartbreaking, humane – and utterly brilliant. These are tough matters to write about with the kind of honesty and authenticity that this writer brings – I think their voice is something really special. It's the story of sisters, one of whom is lost in her own mind, the little pieces of memory and self left floating, untethered; it's a story of a hard-lived life, of the complexities of family and the ways we can damage and be damaged. And yet it is profoundly hopeful about the connection and compassion that can be found even in the most difficult times. Ultimately, it's a story of powerful love.

Stephanie Carty

Davey, Plastic Jesus and the Holy Spirit

'Bad things happen to bad people,' says Pappa as we kneel to pray. He doesn't say what happens to good people like Mamma. Nobody says what happened to her. But I already know.

I press my hands together as tight as I can and sneak a peek at my sister. Jessica thinks God loves her but he gave her curly hair that gets knotted and she can't even see the Holy Spirit like I can.

'What about baby Jesus? It was pretty bad for him in the end, even though he was good.' I hold my arms out to my sides like I'm nailed to wood and roll my eyes back but only cos I know Pappa's eyes are shut. His voice sounds funny these last few weeks, as if he's been gargling with glass.

'Jesus died for our sins, Davey. Remember the special name for the day he died? *Good* Friday. Praise the Lord. He's here in the hour of our need.'

I nod. Jesus looks down from the huge plastic cross on the wall. He winks at me; I wink right back. I guess his superpowers meant the nails didn't hurt. Oh boy, I know how he might have done it! Maybe he had magnetic hands and that's how the nails stayed in, while he tricked the baddies that he was dying. Jesus was good at playing pretend. I am too.

I side-eye Pappa. He strokes his moustache over and over like he's trying to make it feel better. Before we came to live by the church, he wore his plastic suit and special helmet like the rest of us so he didn't look like Pappa at all. But we're safe here: we let our arms and faces go naked. In this hall at the back of the church, the dust is probably hair and skin of holy people, plus little bits of the Body of Christ which is the proper name for the wafers at Mass. We're breathing in the good stuff. It's not being a cannibal or zombie if you're Catholic. I checked. It was worth being whacked just to be sure.

Pappa ends prayer time with 'in the name of the Father, the Son and the Holy Spirit'. There's so much I could tell him but you have to learn the Grown Ups code if you don't want the sting of a belt on the backs of your legs. When they say, 'always tell the truth, boy', what they mean is 'give me the Right Answer', which often times isn't the truth at all. Let's say you start seeing the Holy Spirit. I don't mean imagining it with your eyes screwed up like when you try to picture your guts wriggling under the skin of your belly after you eat, I mean properly see it. The best thing to do is K.I.T.Y. – Keep It To Yourself. I made that up. Plastic Jesus's mouth curled into a smile when I told him that one. The thing is, the Holy Spirit is here just like Pappa said it would be. But he can't see it wrapping around his neck, making his eyes bulge. It's bright yellow. Not daffodil-yellow or crayon-yellow but stare-into-the-sun-till-it-hurts yellow. It doesn't say in the bible but the Holy Spirit sure has a taste! It tastes like when you run your tongue over the bumps of a battery.

Pappa heads off to a meeting with the others who moved here to be with God. I'm stuck with my sister. I whisper *K.I.T.Y.*

'That isn't even a real word,' says Jessica.

'Oh, it's a word just for me. You wouldn't get it.'

She's drawing pictures of Jesus and I don't bother telling her that she's made him look too serious – he's actually a good laugh. The Holy Spirit sneaks up around her and settles in a cloud over her head, changing her hair to a neon-bright shade like the stripes on my old trainers. I rush over to the blinds and shut them to see if Jessica glows in the dark but she ruins it by switching the lamp on next to her. That would be a cool superpower. You could go out in the middle of the night and play hide and seek, looking for the glow. Or read comics under the covers. I blink a couple of times, then the Holy Spirit has disappeared. It'll be back. I'm good at knowing about stuff before it happens. That's why I know where Mamma is. But K.I.T.Y.

When a bad thing happens, sometimes you can try to undo it. Like the first time the Bad Stuff leaked out and nobody on the news told us. They tried to clean it up like nothing ever happened. But people started getting sick. Well, Mamma had spilt red wine on the carpet. It must have been the communion wine, the Blood of Christ. I don't know why she had it, maybe she was keeping it safe for the priest. Anyway, Mamma was on her knees trying to get the stain off the carpet because this place isn't ours and we could get in trouble. We left our old house behind – it wasn't going to be okay for much longer there, not with the Bad Stuff in the air. Mamma scrubbed and scrubbed but that stain was still there, the size of my hand. Pappa was at a meeting. He wasn't going to be happy when he saw that red mark. Mamma rolled back and sat on the heels of her feet like she used to when we played board games back home. I miss the games. Maybe that's why I make up my own now.

'There, that's better,' she said, staring right at the red stain like she couldn't see anything at all. I thought about how maybe it didn't come out because it was Jesus's blood, more special than most. She went out into the yard, just standing there with her arms crossed staring at the sky. I watched the stain as it got bigger: a puddle, wider into a paddling pool, then more and more until the whole carpet was covered like lava. I jumped from the sofa to a chair to the back door using my floor-is-lava skills. I didn't know back then that I saw things no one else did.

'Mamma! Come and see – Jesus's blood is everywhere, like holy lava!'

She squinted at me then turned back to the lake, mumbling that I mustn't talk like that about Jesus, I shouldn't be bus-famous. I ran to her side and leant against her soft arm. I remembered those weeks before we packed up our things and squidged what we could into the car. It was mostly Grown Up things. That was okay, I mean, I'm too old for superhero action figures and I always skipped to the last page in the books Mamma bought me. The old school buses were covered with posters that told us to Stay Safe and to Head to Havens. Everyone looked the same in their all-in-one suits and goggles – like angry bees buzzing about looking for flowers that didn't grow any more. I hated those buses. I hated leaving my mates, my bedroom, my turtle Benji.

The man on the side of the bus had white, white skin and white, white teeth and hair that looked like a wig. He had adverts on TV too. He said that God would look after his people, but he only meant some of the people with the right god, not like my best mate Amir. No way I wanted to be bus-famous, nobody liked that man. Even my dad swore about him once in front of us, said he was a self-serving prick who had no right calling himself a politician. I wrote that backwards for code on my comic so I wouldn't forget.

'Get to bed now, Davey-boy, before your father's back home,' she said. That's when I saw how weird Mamma's eyes had gone. I could see the lake in them. Not just a reflection of the water, I mean they *were* the water – blue waves instead of black dots. She turned away from me, back to the lake. 'The water's safe, you know,' she whispered. But it didn't seem safe, nothing did. I didn't understand what her water-eyes meant but it felt like someone had reached down my throat and squeezed my stomach in their fist.

I never saw Mamma again.

'She's run away from Our Lord,' said Pappa. 'Straight into the hands of the devil and the downfall.'

I never told no one that Mamma didn't run away, that she's in the water.

We sit down for dinner around the little table in the kitchen. *Father, Son, and the Holy Sister*, I think. I must tell Jesus that one later, he'll have a chuckle.

The Holy Spirit is back and stronger than ever. It drips down Pappa, sliding down his skin so it almost looks like it's melting right off like Sunday roast beef from the bone. It's wrapped around Jessica's neck and flows up her nostril each time she breathes in until her nose glows.

'Focus on your food, boy,' snaps Pappa. The bread is not like it was back home – it's flat and dry, out of a plastic packet. W.W.J.D.? What Would Jesus Do – I learnt that at Sunday School, back home. Well, Jesus would turn this rock-bread into soft floury loaves and tasty fishcakes! I stuff a forkful in my mouth and chew it as if it's the nicest thing I've ever tasted, giving my sister a big grin to show my mushed-up food.

'You're gross!' she says, pushing her own plate away.

Pappa slams his fist on the table.

'The Lord has provided and you ungrateful children shame me with your behaviour! Eat your food with humility and the gratitude it deserves.'

I keep my eyes down. That's when it hits me.

The Holy Spirit never comes to me. I turn my left hand over under the table. Not a speck of yellow. Pappa and my sister have the Holy Spirit in their eyeballs. I need to check.

'May I be excused?' I ask. Pappa grunts his reply.

I run to the little mirror in the downstairs bathroom. There's no Holy Spirit in my hair, around my neck. I pull at the skin under each eye. No yellow swimming about, trying to cover up my black dots like the others have. Why does it not want me?

Bad things happen to bad people.

Whatever's happening in our old town, in all the towns, is it going to get me? Maybe God is cross that I haven't been holy enough. Maybe he doesn't like me having fun with Jesus?

I stick my face right up close to the mirror until my breath makes a little cloud. When I rub the smudge away, something has changed. My eyes. They aren't yellow. There are little blue waves inside. Like Mamma's.

I might be a kid but I know what happened. I don't want to know but I know it anyhow. Pappa was mad about the blood-carpet, about the holy wine. He hurt her. The blood pool wasn't Jesus's, it was Mamma's. I saw it before it happened. Then he threw Mamma in the lake.

The water wasn't safe, it was too late for her. Is he going to throw me in, too?

Even though I hear dad shouting for me to come back in for prayers, I ignore him, too busy running out to the lake with Jesus on the plastic cross under my arm.

Mamma wasn't telling me the water was safe for her. She was telling me it was safe for me.

Something's coming and I reckon it's not the Holy Spirit after all.

I push out into the water, my clothes feeling heavier with each step as if they want to pull me down. I can hear Pappa's rough shouting, I can't tell what he's saying no more. I'm up to my waist, my armpits. But the heaviness pulls me down. A glug of water gets into my mouth and I sick it back up. *The water is safe, the water is safe.*

My legs hurt and I realise I've never tried to swim with clothes on, it's too hard. I'm so tired. I want to sleep, to stop, to sink under and find Mamma at the bottom of the lake. The water sucks at me, sings to me. The cross bobs on a wave, I turn it over and look straight at Jesus. His arms are out wide as usual, as if he's saying *let me carry you*. I fling myself on top of the cross and wriggle out of my trousers. He holds me. I close my eyes and float. I squeeze them so tight. I don't open them even when there's a flash of light so bright my eyelids feel burnt, the taste of metal stronger than ever, one million batteries stuffed into my mouth. I hold tight onto Jesus and know that in three days' time they'll find us, as if we've come back from the dead.

STEPHANIE CARTY is a writer, NHS consultant clinical psychologist and trainer in Gloucestershire, UK. Her short fiction is widely published. She has been shortlisted for competitions including the Bristol Short Story Prize, Aesthetica Creative Writing Award and Bridport Prize. Her novella-in-flash *Three Sisters of Stone* won Best Novella in the Saboteur Awards. Her writers' craft book *Inside Fictional Minds: Tips from Psychology for Creating Characters* was published by Ad Hoc Fiction in 2021.

SECOND PRIZE
Comments from judge Norah Perkins

This story is electric and brutal and funny and sad – a real tour de force, that gets the combination of dystopia, horror and the uncanny familiar just right, and leaves you at the edge of your seat. The ending is unexpected and ultimately very moving. Although it leaves you gut-punched, the child narrator's voice absolutely crackles with energy and fierce humour – I would love to have spent more time with them…

Kristen Loesch

Important Letters

People get restless at the assisted-living home while waiting to die so the nurses ask me if I will give weekly calligraphy lessons to the ones still holding on. To paintbrushes. They say they've seen me in the art room writing such lovely letters to my son. I possess excellent fine motor skills, in fact. Doctor says there's nothing wrong with my sight my hearing my hands my breaths, there's only something a little wrong with me. Mory. Breaks and starts; things missing. In the first lesson I tell everyone I haven't been properly trained in the art of calligraphy and all they're seeing is just Chinese. They smile patiently at me all they see is just Chinese.

*

The nurses give us something for the pain. T. Not real bamboo brushes, but brushes from a child's art supply kit that have big handles and a rounded tip so you don't feel it.

It is important to make each stroke in a single motion, without lifting your hand. Somebody asks where to begin. I say people begin with birth: 1932, I am born on the fourth day of the fourth month to a pretty fourth wife in Shanghai, but the number four is unlucky, sounds like the word for death, si, a spitting sound, a hiss, like the sky bristling over the East China Sea before a typhoon, like my mother crying without moving her mouth.

*

You might think most of us are too old to make any mark, but the others rip their paper, use too much force. This is what it looks like when people use too much fource: 1946 – I run away – with a stolen mahjong set – ivory tiles, like clenched teeth – get as far the red-light district of Hongkew, red is lucky – I stay flat on my back, let my thoughts fall away – I'm lying next to no one I'm lying to no one I am no one. One day something else falls away, lands with a splash in the chamber pot – plenty of red – it's ugly – oily –flat flounder's head – reedy limbs – eyes like my mother's – casket is the mahjong box with the sliding – wooden – cover.

Rip, rip, r—i—p.

I write to my son: Do you remember that traditional Chinese writing is supposed to stay *vertical*, never horizontal? But of course you remember. You remem. You reme. You r me.

*

All of us in here have gone through too much. Paper, so I teach the others how to hold their brushes correctly, lighter, higher, upright. Spine straight, shoulders back, legs together like they've never been apart. 1949, the Communist Revolution, I get a one-way ticket to America. I board the ship, sew myself back together on the journey. Up, out, pull, up, out, pull, see now you've got the strokes in order, now you've made a character. This is the character: A young woman all alone in a foreign country. She meets an American man who likes everything brand-new. Lucky him. She's so new she doesn't even have a birth certificate.

She makes up a fake birthday, third day of the third month this time. She gets married, but in America the Chinese wife of a white man is less than the fourth wife of her father. Her mouth begins to rot from too many fake smiles. The doctors say she can't have children, too damaged, maybe too skinny. The grains of hope she catches between her chopsticks are too small to eat.

I tell the others: Careful not to keep too much in. K on the brush. It will drip when you're not looking. And always remember: *vertical!* You cannot just cross. The page. Things out. An ocean.

*

My only child my son my sweet *bao bei*,
are
you
staying
vertical
or
are
you
horizontal?

*

I explain to the others that if they leave off even one tiny stroke, the entire meaning will change, because there are smaller wor(l)ds hidden within every character. Imagine for example if *four* became *for*. Forget. Forward.

The others shrug because they are only in this place to pass. The time. During our 'calligraphy hour' I wander the room; I look over shoulders. 1973, I am divorced, working as a waitress, better to be on my feet all day than being off them, like in the only other job I ever held; I look over shoulders. I see empty plates, full stomachs, perfectly round bellies. There's a Chinese girl who comes in often, befriends me, says her ex-boyfriend turned out to be married. Now she plans to give the baby up, go to college. She asks if I want a baby. I say yes but I've been too scar(r)ed. Yes, but (k)now you're okay, she says. (K)Now you're okay.

*

I write to my son: I think I have left off one tiny stroke.

I try to find it sometimes but it's too well hidden so I break every memory I have into smaller pieces, look at them closely, like I remember I taught you how to write in Chinese too even though you'd always complain *come on Ma I'm dying of boredom!* I remember I told you to be careful because the characters look hardy but they're so fragile as they grow bigger, it's easy to go too fast, to go outside the lines, off the edge, to spill out everywhere, onto the sidewalk into the gutters all over your mother's hands. I remember but I cannot redo cannot replace cannot

return
turn
urn.

My beautiful child I'm sorry for making you die of fourdom. You never visit me here, are you mad? E-up? If you won't come to me then I'll have to go to you! Some of me is gone and the rest of me is going. Soon, I just have to give a calligraphy lesson first, have to teach all the others how to start over.

KRISTEN LOESCH is an Asian-American writer based in the Pacific Northwest. She placed runner-up in the 2019 Mslexia Short Story Competition and the Funny Pearls Short Story Competition 2020. Her short fiction can be found or is forthcoming in *SmokeLong Quarterly, CRAFT, Fractured Lit, FlashBack Fiction, Barren Magazine, Lunate, Timeworn Literary Journa*l, and others. She is represented by Zeitgeist Agency. She lives with her husband and children.

Third Prize

Comments from judge Norah Perkins

I loved this story. The writer has that rare ability to – with the lightest touch – show me not just one woman's whole life in a glimpse, but also how loss works – loss of memories, of abilities, of history, of place, of those we love… And formally, it was beautifully done, the dropping out of letters and of meaning and memory echoing each other. Just a very burnished, beautiful story, with immense but subtle power.

Lynda Mason

The Great Pretender

Tyler settled the crown more comfortably and picked up a black bag. These golden pieces of cardboard were ten for a pound at Savacentre so he rarely ran low, but he'd had a run of bad luck lately. One had fallen into a puddle on Tuesday. On Wednesday, the Gough twins had shoved him aside and thrown that day's crown into the railway embankment. Powerlessly, he had watched his treasure wheeling through the ash-grey sky in a gleaming arc, coming to rest on a pile of used syringes. Last night a seagull had shat on one. Now, he had only the one currently on his head.

Depositing his bin bag into the communal bay, Tyler shuffled towards the strip of shops on Blackwell Road. He felt acutely that he *was* shuffling and was ashamed and self-conscious. His head hang low.

Moving into the concrete underpass, he glanced warily around him and frowned at the orange and black graffiti sprayed generously across the damp walls. Although he hated this tunnel and had been tripped, kicked and shoved in it many a time, it was nevertheless part of his domain and he didn't want fear to rule over any of it. Standing taller and pulling his faded purple coat tightly against him, he descended.

Mira saw him approaching like the weird zombie he was and rolled her eyes. Tyler lived on benefits and was unlikely to have much cash to take or scam. He had been robbed a few times she knew but to the local thugs it was just not worth the effort these days. So he passed through the neighbourhood largely unmolested apart from the milder forms of assault. Mira wondered if he wore his crown in bed. The thought made her smile.

'Your Highness,' Mira's voice echoed around the fetid space, and she bowed sarcastically.

Tyler looked nervously at her but gave a wan smile. It was so rare that his subjects noticed him. He knew he was a weak king and he had no advisors to help him. This was a real red-letter day. He nodded graciously.

'Got any cash?' she asked, holding out her hand hopefully.

Tyler slowly shook his head. 'Only this for new crowns,' he replied, holding out a grubby coin. Mira considered snatching it but couldn't help feeling a twinge of something uncomfortable when she peered up into his anxious face. 'Go on then, go get your crowns, my man!'

She laughed and the sound clung to him like a ghost, all the way to the end of the dark, dripping footpath.

Half an hour later, his figure shambled past in the opposite direction. Mira was half-way through a soggy joint and almost didn't notice anything amiss until he'd passed her by. Suddenly she realised he was bare-headed.

'Oi!' she yelled, angling her head sarcastically. 'Is that skanky store no longer stocking fine goooold crowns?'

He turned slightly and she gasped as her eyes rested on the two thin rivulets of bright blood running through his grizzled hair and into his mouth. His eye was bloodshot and swollen.

'Bloody hell. What happened to you?'

There was a long pause. 'I'm a bad king,' Tyler said in quiet despair.

'You've lost me.'

'That's what *they* all say,' and he waved his arms to encompass the world – out there. Throwing up his grazed hands, Mira could see he was shaking.

'It got thrown away, as punishment,' and he rubbed his head as if to check his crown really had been lost. 'Then they came back for the pound,' he added. Leaning heavily against the wall, Tyler said slowly, carefully, 'I'm not who anyone would choose.'

'Yeah, well that's not how it works is it? You're born to it.'

The sound of dripping reverberated through the tunnel, its regular rhythm seeming to mark the seconds ticking by.

Tyler's hands twitched as if he was desperately grasping on to this thought. 'Right!' His voice faded and he lost himself for a moment. 'But I don't remember how it happened now. And he was always the best one.'

Mira stood up and shook the life back into her legs. 'You can't have two kings, moron. Especially in this one, crappy neighbourhood.' She sighed. 'I'll walk with you a bit, you look wobbly.'

'I'm not good on my feet lately,' he admitted.

'Got any food at home?' she asked. 'Caviar *will* do.'

Ruefully, Tyler just shook his head.

'Servants letting you down, are they?' She winked. At this he smiled weakly and nodded.

Standing outside his mouldering flat, Mira stared, appalled at the jagged glass in the peeling window frames and the spray-painted door. The word 'RETARD' in large black letters covered nearly the door's whole surface. Some joker had drawn a crown symbol above this and in smaller letters written in another hand were the words, 'By royal appointment to a nonce'.

'Jesus,' she said as Tyler unlocked the door.

'I have tea?' he said hopefully as she followed him. 'No milk though. I only get milk on Wednesdays when Mrs Evans comes.'

'That your carer?'

Tyler shook his head firmly. 'Psychologist,' he said.

Pushing him onto a sagging chair, she peered into his face. 'I'll get a cloth then we'll have some disgusting black tea, alright?'

Tyler seemed not to hear, although he appeared content enough. There was a pause and then the sound of rummaging and clattering from the kitchen. Mira came back into the room, stretching herself. She glanced around.

'Your clocks' stopped,' she said flatly, pointing to a gaily painted cuckoo clock in the corner. Tyler nodded. Mira felt herself becoming irritated.

'Also, your cups and plates are all cracked, and your sink's blocked. I daren't even think what your toilet's like,' she said sternly. 'You live worse than I do'.

Wiping his face carefully with damp kitchen roll, she stomped off to brave the bathroom, returning with a half-used tube of Germolene and a grim look.

'Just as I thought,' she said.

As Mira leant over him, they could hear faintly below children's shouts and the ring of a bicycle bell.

'What do you do as king anyway?' she asked. 'Do you give speeches? If so, you could start with those little buggers below. They're always racing through that bloody tunnel and running over my stuff. And my legs sometimes,' she continued, wincing.

Tyler reflected for a moment. 'I did, at the beginning. But nobody listened. He was the orator,' and he nodded vaguely in the direction of the clock.

'Big talker, was he?'

Tyler grinned.

'So, who was he then, this second king?' asked Mira curiously.

'He was the sun,' Tyler said simply.

Mira stood and looked at him, frowning. She shook her head angrily. 'What am I doing here with your craziness?' she asked the world, hands in the air. There was no response to this. Putting the top back on the cream, she vanished. Five minutes later the sound of a kettle could be heard hissing and fizzing.

When she returned, Tyler was hanging up his purple coat and counting the ornaments on his mantelpiece.

'Kettle's on,' she said, then paused. 'You do know you've got a shit ton of meds in that bathroom cabinet? Do you even know what you should be taking?'

He turned and nodded. 'Yes. Three green pills in the morning, two pink-blue striped ones at night.'

'What about the white ones in the jar?'

'As and when?' Tyler said hesitatingly. Looking down he seemed to realise that wasn't quite right. 'No, those are for *after* dinner.' His face still looked like a question mark.

'Jesus,' Mira said again, under her breath.

She took a stroll around the front room. Everything was dusty but the furniture was solid and of good quality. There were travel themed knick-knacks dotted around and colourful paintings on the walls. Splashes of vibrant blues and scarlets contrasted sharply with the drab world outside. Mira stopped in front of a heavy, mahogany cabinet. 'This cupboard's locked,' she said, 'bloody great padlock on it! Is this where you keep the crown jewels?' Chuckling at her own joke, she leant towards the lock and gave it a tug. Tyler came over in a rush, stumbling over the rug.

'No, no,' and he held his head and seemed distressed. 'Just safekeeping.'

The kettle clicked.

'Tea's up,' Mira said.

Mira found herself back at Tyler's flat the next day. For half an hour, just to check. Yet somehow, as the days went by, she found herself stopping in each afternoon. They would sip rancid tea and watch TV. She read all his medication labels and wrote instructions, pinning an A4 sheet to the sticky fridge. Bottles of out-of-date pills were thrown away and rooms were slowly cleaned and aired. On Wednesdays, she sat and observed his visitor. Tyler never objected. He seemed to take things all in his stride. That first Wednesday, Mrs Evans had brought along some groceries and a new set of crowns.

'Strange kind of psychologist,' she murmured.

'I'm an outreach worker,' Mrs Evans explained with a smile, 'so a bit of everything really. We have a small budget to get him a couple of things. He has a tendency to forget to eat sometimes.'

'I'm not surprised, being doped up on all those pills,' Mira replied hotly.

The older woman sighed. 'Yes, I know. We have applied for more help for him as things aren't improving. Hopefully, that shouldn't take many more weeks.'

'How long has he been like this?' Mira asked curiously.

'A year now, must be,' Mrs Evans replied sadly. Then she hesitated, looking shyly at Mira's faded and dirty clothes. 'But you look like you could do with help yourself, lovey. I can refer you if you like?'

'Not bloody likely,' Mira snapped. 'I'm not turning into the walking dead. I'm just in a slump.'

'Temporary,' she added.

Mrs Evans did not pursue the subject.

Eight Weeks Later

As the sun set over the sprawling estate, glowing plumes of light were illuminating the front room and sparking dust motes into a last joyful frenzy. Mira and Tyler were sitting together companionably, drinking milky tea and eating digestives.

'Tell me about him,' Mira said quietly.

It had been such a short time, yet Tyler had already lost quite a lot of his vague, shaggy look and he seemed far more alert. Certainly, he'd had a shave. Today's crown was exactly in place, blazing in those final rays of sunlight and exactly in centre place on his head. Even his purple coat appeared to have had a brush.

He hesitated, his mouth full of crumbs. 'I could show you?' He twitched in his chair nervously, but the look in his dark eyes was steady.

Mira nodded.

Retrieving a small key from under an ornament, Tyler crossed to the heavy cupboard.

Out came an assortment of long robes in different colours, a large scrapbook and two photograph albums, the most recent of which was packed with loose photos and newspaper cuttings. Between them they lifted everything onto the kitchen table. Mira sifted carefully through the scrapbook. 'He was an actor!' she exclaimed in excitement.

'Yes!' nodded Tyler, breaking into a smile. 'He was like ... the sun,' he continued helplessly, 'everything he touched he lit up.'

Mira gazed at the clippings of reviews and interviews with local reporters for a few minutes before moving on to the photo albums. The first was very neat and organised, photos arranged by date and with comical captions underneath. Childhood poses and scenes of amateur dramatic performances. Shots of what appeared to be more professional plays and rehearsals and then snaps of Tyler started appearing in the record. Tyler on his own smiling widely on a beach, Tyler with a glass of wine laughing into the camera. Tyler and this other man, arms around each other by a Christmas tree, at a food market, in the Canadian Rockies. Under each photograph was smartly printed the place and the date and then a line that said simply, 'The Kings!'

The final image was of the two men in a bar, glasses chinking. 'The King and I!' read the caption.

Mira felt she was hardly breathing. 'A silly thing,' said Tyler softly, by her side. 'A bit of fun.'

The second album contained a few random photos. The two of them posing, both tanned and beshaded in Barcelona, later in Rome. Next, some loose theatre tickets. Mostly however, it seemed to contain small clippings. Mira picked one up at random.

'Police are no nearer to an arrest after the murder of local actor Arran Rex, 45, who was stabbed to death in the doorway of Blaze nightclub in the early hours of Saturday morning.

Police are keeping an open mind as to the motive. Anyone with information is urged to contact Hendon CID immediately. Meanwhile, Arran's partner Tyler Royal, 46, remains in a stable condition in hospital.'

Silence filled the room. The sun dipped below the horizon and darkness descended like a shroud. Mira dropped the clipping and looked wide-eyed at Tyler, who had placed his crown gently on the table. 'We really *were* kings,' he said sadly.

Lynda Mason writes short stories that aim to give a voice to the people in our society who feel lonely or disconnected. Occasionally her tales take on a magical twist that is often as much of a surprise to the author as to the reader. Lynda is currently writing a young adult novel. She lives in Birmingham and can mostly be found buried under a pile of books.

Highly Commended
Comments from judge Norah Perkins

This is such a lovely story – of a real odd couple, who embody grace and humanity and humour and compassion despite the challenges they both face in their lives. And it cleverly turns – just at the end – into something so unexpectedly moving, and deftly rearranges all your assumptions…

Note: The BSSA team also awarded the Acorn Award for an unpublished story to The Great Pretender.

Linda Wang

Ma's Favourite

It's her fourteenth day in hospital and I don't need to imagine how she's doing any more. I have been handed an iPad in what looks like a sandwich bag and when I tap the screen, the live feed from the ward comes into focus.

At first, I don't spot the body. Then something thrums and I see the juddering rise and fall of a chest swaddled in hospital sheets. White tubing reaches into the throat and every vein seems to be growing a cannula and extension line. All these machines, they look more like they're sucking the life out of her than keeping her alive.

I can't picture this body as my Ma. This isn't the Ma who made me mooncakes every mid-autumn after my favourite flavours sold out, or who taught me the importance of eating lo bak go – radish cake – over New Year. This isn't the Ma who despaired whenever aunties and uncles joked about my broken Cantonese, or who spent hours, once, laying into my teachers after the other kids laughed at my almond eyes.

Through the screen, the nurse's words sound far away, like the last fading moments of a dream before you wake.

'There's been no improvement yet,' the nurse says, 'but we're doing everything we can for your mum.'

On my way home, I pass through Chinatown to buy pork knuckles and sweet vinegar. As I walk along Gerrard Street, I stop at the windows of each restaurant and practise reading the dim sum menus written in Chinese. A few of the photos are incorrectly labelled and it throws me off. I open my language app to double-check. Sometimes, it feels more like I'm learning a series of shapes than individual words.

At one restaurant, I finally get all the names right. The evening is cool and my jumper is too thin to stop goosebumps forming. Cyclists pass by me, carrying on their backs large black boxes filled with favourite dishes that people have missed whilst stuck at home. A group of boys collect their takeaway orders and walk off, laughing and shoving each other as they go.

The first time the other kids made it clear I wasn't one of them was the day I brought beef lo mein into school for lunch. I still don't know what they took offence to specifically. I only remember all my food ending up on my head, and going hungry, hiding behind the games shed in the playground, with bits of carrot, beansprout and meat congealing in my hair. After that, I begged Ma to let me eat fish fingers and shepherd's pie from the school canteen. It was many years later that I finally understood just how much this must have hurt her, to see a part of me so cruelly erased. But eventually Ma said yes, so my name became the target of their jibes instead.

An elderly man is smoking outside the supermarket and I bow my head to him. Pink crates are lined up by the shopfront as usual, but where they once held mounds of rambutan, jackfruit and guava, only a few sad apples half-fill them now. Inside, I place ginger in my basket, sniffing for freshness first, then head to aisle four to pick up my vinegar. I choose the biggest knuckles from the fridge at the back of the store.

Pork knuckles with ginger and sweet vinegar is Ma's favourite and I have finally, at the tender age of thirty-one, learned how to make it. I hope to have it perfected by the time Ma comes home.

A woman in a maroon tunic mistakes me for someone competent and starts reeling off sentence after sentence in Cantonese at me. She might be telling me there's a special offer on or something, but all I can hear are sounds I really should know the meaning of, and the occasional word I recognise cutting in between like there's a poor connection on a videocall. I start to form an answer in my head, but I can't get the word order right. I give up after three attempts. My mangled Cantonese will be a spotlight on my London upbringing, exposing me as a fraud. So I tell her in English that I'm sorry, but I'm actually Korean. I pay and leave quickly.

As I go, the vinegar sloshes in the bottle and the plastic bag thuds against my thigh. The handles start to stretch and they dig into my fingers. I walk under the tall, ornate gate by Wan Chai at the end of Gerrard Street, past the bakery Ma and I usually buy pandan rolls and pineapple buns from, and head down Newport Court, where all the bubble tea shops seem to be popping up.

Then I see them. That same group of boys again.

Ma likes to joke that I've become more British than Chinese, but over these past few months, I have never been made to feel more Chinese than I do now. Strangers in the street have started shouting at me to go home. They seem more certain about my identity than I am. I still don't know how to feel about this. It was only today I read on Twitter that a Thai man in San Francisco was murdered last night.

The boys spot me now and I know how this will end.

One shouts: 'Fuck off, Chinese virus.'

'We don't want you in our country,' says another. He throws the empty chow mein box he is holding to the ground and launches at me.

The first hit cracks my cheekbone. The bottle of vinegar smashes when I fall and the glass cuts my hand. There are four of them now. They stand in the vinegar and stamp on me so hard they leave sticky, black footprints all over. Their kicks develop a rhythm. I feel the pork knuckles bump against my side and, without thinking, I reach out and grab them. I make myself very small, and with every kick and punch, I hug these chunks of flesh, skin and bone tighter and tighter and tighter, and even as my arms buckle and bruise, I still can't bear to let go.

Eventually, the blue lights scatter my assailants and a paramedic helps me up. I sit on the ambulance steps holding the pork knuckles across my lap. Safe in the plastic bag, they're the only things not covered in blood. The paramedic doesn't try to take them from me. Blood drips from a large gash above my left eye. It gels my lashes together and my eye sticks when I blink. The paramedic applies gauze to the wound and, suddenly, I wish I was eight again, and in Saturday school, where I made my classmates laugh with silly faces behind our teachers' backs, and where I drew tails and long noses on the pictures of boys and girls in my Chinese textbook. I imagine what might have been, if only I had spent hours practising the stroke orders and pronunciation of each and every Chinese character instead. Would I have ended up here tonight? Feeling not quite Chinese, but not quite British either?

'Don't worry, darling, we'll get you patched up in no time.'

It takes me a moment to realise the paramedic is speaking to me. She smiles at me like a spoonful of sugar helps the medicine go down and I can't believe that anyone could think that wounds like these can be fixed so easily.

I tighten my grip around the pork knuckles, but the bones dig into the cuts on my hand, and it stings all over.

LINDA WANG qualified as a veterinary surgeon from the University of Edinburgh. She left clinical practice at the beginning of 2021 and now works as a medical writer in London. Earlier this year, she was shortlisted for New Writing North's A Writing Chance 2021. She is currently studying on the Faber Academy's Writing a Novel course and is attempting to finish her novel featuring a veterinary surgeon protagonist, about loneliness, burnout and female friendship.

HIGHLY COMMENDED
Comments from judge Norah Perkins

This story feels utterly relevant today, the story of a young woman who experiences the kind of racism and violence that end up as the news items we glance over every day on Twitter. It's human and intimate and painful and beautifully observed.

Ruth Bateson

The Pheasant

As she makes her way through the paddock, it strikes her – how old and ridiculous she must look, struggling up the gentle slope, her whole body listing to the left, as though there was a great headwind. The day has been still, with a pewter cast. Dour. Her lips purse around the shape of the word. The ground is already pale with frost, the long grass shushing against her trouser legs.

She pauses and looks back to a low white house that sits hunched against the winter fields. She'd come too far to go back for her boots now. Her lungs are tight with the cold air, her throat rasping a little from shouting out Ash's name. Damn dog. She presses on.

The fence at the top end of the paddock had been replaced in June, the wood still bright and raw-looking. The new gate did not hang well – the Hawkins brothers had made a mess of setting the new fence-posts, and the over-gate latch would embed itself in the soft grain of the wood. She leans into the gate with her shoulder and tries to loosen the metal fastening, her gloved fingers slipping. She curses sharply and steps back to catch her breath. Pulls off her gloves and makes starfish shapes in the air with her hands, frowning at the tight, swollen flesh around her fingers, the grotesque curl of them.

Leaning back into the gate, she curses the Hawkins brothers, and she curses herself for letting Karen take over the summer work. While she's at it, she curses the delivery man from Isherwoods, Dr Aslam from the rheumatology centre, and the awful blonde woman at Naylors. She is cursing the whole sorry lot of them when the latch suddenly gives way, and the gate swings open. She stumbles forward and is immediately struck in the chest by the gate falling back on itself.

Oh! she says, stunned, and then she crumples and begins to wheeze with laughter. She finds a tissue in her pocket to dab at her eyes and remembers the great heaving slope of Clem's shoulders as he laughed. Those early mornings when they'd first moved in, mugs of tea on the back step, Clem in his faded blue overalls, the birds in the flowering currant hedge already busy with their day. Was that when he started calling her 'sparrow'? Like Piaf? she'd asked. Christ, no! he'd said – had she not heard herself singing?

She leaves the lopsided gate hanging, and walks across a narrow, scrubby strip of land towards the wood. It was in the dog's nature to chase things; he would always be drawn there. She gives a low whistle and pictures him loping from the trees, breath steaming.

At the edge of the wood, blackthorn branches catch at her coat sleeves and hair. She keeps to the faint path but is careful with her feet; the uneven ground is a tangle of roots. Spindly saplings reach up out of the leaf litter – hazel, elder and silver birch. It had always been called Pyll Wood; the Suttons had a name for every corner. And the bluebells – the bluebells! Enough to make a grown man swoon, Clem had said. Come May, you couldn't tell where the sky ended and the bluebells began.

She calls the dog and feels the quiet of the trees crowding in. She tries again, a little louder, and turns, imagines flash of pale fur between the birches, but it is nothing.

The light is draining from the day now, bluish shadows thickening. She will need to turn back soon. She continues down the path until the trees thin out a little and red flares of new growth are revealed. She stops at a pile of brushwood, pulls off a glove and puts out her hand as though to pat it. Clem used to gather up the coppiced branches, bringing home withered leaves in his hair and pockets. She lowers her hand to the papery bark.

A faint rustling sound disturbs her – but when she opens her eyes, she can't be sure if it was a sound at all, because she feels it under her skin. She turns a slow circle, squinting into the dark spaces between the trees.

Ash! she calls sharply. She is filling her lungs to call a second time, when a terrible explosion of feathers and flapping from the nearby brambles has her clutching her throat in fright. She steps back, but the ground seems to buckle beneath her feet, and by the time she recognises the panicked *ack-ack!* call of the pheasant, it is too late. She considers the strange angles of her limbs as they move through space, and just before the earth rises up to meet her, just before her head snaps back to meet the root of an elder tree, a childhood memory of swing boats comes to her in a giddy scarlet blur.

She can taste iron. Earth and blood. A dull throbbing at the back of her head. She makes a weak fist with her left hand and tries to push herself up; manages to raise her head a little, attempts to lift a shoulder, then a scalding pain rushes through her and she drops back into the leaf-litter, gasping. A sourness prickles at her throat and she spits out grit and bile. Her stupid right hand curled in the dirt.

She lies still. Breathes around the pain cradled in her pelvis, feels the darkness pressing in like a blanket. A thin trail of liquid cools on her chin as she listens to the soft hiss and rattle of her breath. A lattice of tree branches reveals itself to her, etched in shades of blue-black. She can see that the night is punctured with pin-pricks of light. I am seeing stars, she thinks, trying to swallow down a hiccough of laughter, wary of the spasm of her ribs.

When Karen was a child, she couldn't sleep with the curtains closed. The night sky seemed to settle her; she was fascinated by the fattening moon. Even in the dark, you could make out the stubborn tilt of her chin, the blunt shine of her hair. It is strange; though her daughter calls by almost every day, with offerings – a packet of fuses, a bag of porridge oats, a bunch of hothouse daffodils – she cannot picture Karen's adult face; just the shape of her through the warped glass of the front door. The way she had been holding herself lately; the sharp angles of her shoulders, everything taut with concern. Oh, Karen. You'll be so cross with me.

The few remaining leaves on the trees seem to crackle in the cold night air. She listens for signs of nocturnal life, but can hear nothing but the stop-start chatter of her own teeth. She wonders what happened to the pheasant – maybe it is roosting nearby. Such ridiculous creatures – all that useless, exotic plumage. Like those two handsome birds Clem had hung from a nail in the back porch once, all the brightness gone from their eyes. They'll hang for a few days, he'd said. You're not going soft on me, Maggs, are you? And she'd said no, but I'm not plucking the buggers either. A warm spell – it must have been – the maggots fell from them after just two days.

The last of the pheasants. She smiles carefully. Tries to concentrate on the needling stars, the constellation of her daughter's freckles. But sometimes the pain flushes through her with its ugly heat; sometimes she is nothing but a vessel for it, her skin stretched thin around it. The push and pull of it makes her brittle and weary.

She is cast up. The cold is in her bones now. The frost has made a delicate lace about her cuffs and hair. She wants to curl up in the leaf-litter, but her limbs are made of cardboard. She watches Clem as he takes off his cap and joins her on the back step, the warm smell of work on him. There is a flurry of soft brown feathers from a flowering currant bush; there is chirruping and twittering, and then it is gone. Dawn spreads like thin blue milk and there is a dog, running through the trees.

RUTH BATESON grew up in rural Shropshire and currently lives and works in Bristol. Obsessed with words and pictures, Ruth has always written, but in recent years her collection of notebooks has expanded. She has been focusing on short fiction to explore ideas and to develop her skills as a writer. 'The Pheasant' is her first published work.

LOCAL PRIZE
Comments by BSSA Team

We loved the liminal quality of this story: as day fades to evening a woman crosses the fields to the dark woods, in search of her lost dog. Above all, it is an poignant discovery of the fine balance between life and death, as seen from the women's perspective and in a voice that is both unsentimental yet emotionally compelling.

Rosaleen Lynch

Hail

Raindrops don't float, in puddles, on ponds and not on the waves of the sea, is what you say when I say it's raining; it's hail, you say as white beads bounce on tarpaulin, as if we ripped off a floatation block and clawed at the polystyrene, which now gathers in the wooden recesses and joints of the boat, tiny unpolished pearls, shucked from the oyster sky, like when we were kids and watched hailstones, starting small, get bigger, to the size of grapefruit, dropping like bombs in a summer storm, which no one at school notices until car alarms go off and glass smashes outside and the teacher won't let us out, and it's over and she retrieves a stone and cuts it open to show us the rings inside, one for every time the hailstone fell and rose in the cycle of precipitation, she says, a rare beauty, wishing she'd had a camera to capture what others may not believe and in college when we read Shakespeare, you and I remember that day, when Antony asks Cleopatra if her love for him has grown cold and she answers, 'Ah, dear, if I be so, from my cold heart let heaven engender hail, and poison it in the source, and the first stone drop in my neck' and 'as it determines, so dissolve my life!' and now you say it's hail, as the shadow of the shower passes over the boat and we watch this lone cloud move out to sea and wait for the hailstones to change from frosted white to clear and melt and disappear but they turn to, it looks like glass, and roll atop the tarpaulin and in the bottom of the boat they tinkle as they collide and I bend down, scoop some up and examine them in my gloved hand where they roll and lie in the creases but don't melt, and I pull off my other glove with my teeth, fish-blood tasting copper, tip the beads into my naked hand but they don't melt, just lie, moving with the roll of the sea, marbles the size of tears and I hold them out for you, to take in your cupped hands, in case mine were cold but yours shake and drop them, into a shoe you kicked off earlier and I place my hand under yours and catch the rest and pour them into the open wrist of my empty glove, the tips of the fingers filling up and I wipe beads from the tarpaulin into the glove and you help me scoop some up from the bottom of the boat until the thumb grows full and the wrist begins to swell and spill because there are too many to fit in while the timber grooves of the boat floor harbour a dotted line of tears and I turn to the seawater and dip my net to fill the fish buckets to the brim, with what you say now is not hail, but neither is it a gathering of polystyrene beads, pearls, marbles or glass, none of these would fall from the sky, you say, and I wonder if it's salt and put one in my mouth and though it's salty, it does not dissolve when I grind it between back teeth, like a silver-ball cake decoration, waiting for the shell to crack but my molar gives way first and a tooth fragment I pick off with my tongue, enormous in my mouth is a speck between my fingers, and I flick it off and swallow, though I don't mean to and imagine the worst that is yet to come, and the cloud comes back and in its shadow, as the hail had fallen, it rises again, from the sea, buckets and boat floor, fish turning tail up rise into the sky, as does my filled glove, fingers first and your shoe, toe pointing high and the boat tips up at the front and you look down at me without surprise as I lie in my open grave looking up until I drop again when beads pop out from between the timber joints and the boat rocks, tilts me forward and back; a swing-boat pulled by ropes I could not pull and my rib cage lifts in pain, contracts and my connected bones and flesh follow me up out of the boat, my chest tightening as if winched up by a crane into the cloud but nothing holds me there, facing skyward, my body carried on a cradle draft of air, I wonder how I must look to you below in the boat, this human puppet on a string of pain, a cheap movie effect sucked up into a CGI sunset as more beads join the cloud, and gather on my chest over pain, soothing, connecting, magnetised, oil drops fusing into slick, hailstones melting to form a pool where my chest becomes water clear and I can see through layers of my clothes, to my breast, to my rib cage and my heart inside and there above my beating heart, lodged in the bottom of my oesophagus, is the bead, a bullet, the clarity surrounding it turns a bleeding opaque red and my tears drop down from the cloud into the sea, a hailstone shower of salt diamonds for you my love, still in the same boat as I grow cold, though my love for you does not, as Cleopatra tells Antony, if it's true my love for you grows cold, let my heart grow hailstone and let the first one drop down my throat to dissolve my life and the next smite my child and the next my children one by one until all of my people are killed by the pellet storm, but I tell you, my heart does not grow cold, it's another's and you can't hear me, through the hail of bullets, as we lie together, sheltering under an English Lit class table, a lifeboat that saves just one of us from the storm, but listen, I tell you now, my love, not to let your own heart grow cold, it is the cold hearted who produce the plagues of pellets that kill us all, instead, we must use the salt of our tears to preserve life, and if nothing else, to lower the temperature at which hearts freeze.

Rosaleen Lynch, an Irish youth and community worker and writer in the East End of London with words in lots of lovely places, some on longlists and shortlists, some winning, waiting and forthcoming, and can be found on Twitter @quotes_52 and 52Quotes.blogspot.com.

Catherine Smith

Jellyfish

You're slicing onions when Emily's text pings. White letters on a black background. *10 pm to collect? I'll have a taxi waiting. Hope that's OK.*

No kisses, of course. Not even her initial. You type, *Fine. I'll have your stuff ready.*

You hesitate. *Stuff?* Shouldn't that be *worldly goods* or *precious possessions*? Emily works in Marketing. She's always teased you about your 'cautious' vocabulary. But no point, now, trying to please her. You press send and take a large swig from your glass of Merlot, then go back to slicing the onions. Emily hated slicing onions. They made her weep. An onion's defence mechanism produces an irritating chemical, propanethial s-oxide, meant to stop the plant being consumed by pests. Once it's released, it quickly evaporates, finds its way into eyes and dissolves in the surface water to form sulphenic acid. This irritates the lacrimal – tear – gland. It affects some people, but not others. Onions have never made you cry.

Three evenings ago, as you sat opposite each other at the kitchen table, Emily sobbed as she confessed to an affair which had been going on for five months. She was so sorry, but this person – *Dana* – was just the most amazing woman she'd ever met and she couldn't go on pretending everything between the two of you was OK.

You felt sick, and miserable, but you weren't shocked. You watched her lips move, and desperately wanted to kiss her, so she'd have to stop talking, and the soreness in your chest would ease and this horrible thing she was telling you wouldn't be true. She told you she was going to move out that evening, and that you could decide which of your shared possessions to keep and which she could have, because that was only fair. You let her finish talking and crying. You both agreed she would pay her share of the rent and bills until the end of the month, then you'd take on the tenancy yourself. She said it wasn't your fault, it was hers. She'd changed, you hadn't. You wanted to scream, *change back and love me again because I still love you and this Dana can fuck off, you can forget her.*

But you said nothing more. You sat in the kitchen as she packed, called a taxi, left. Then you stripped all the bedding, shoved it into the washing machine and selected the hottest programme.

After washing up, you wonder about having some time to yourself before you decide what to give Emily. But there's nothing you want to watch on TV or Netflix. You and Emily had been watching the latest series of *Killing Eve*; or rather, you realise now, you'd been watching. She'd been staring through the window, fiddling with her hair.

You dig out four Bags for Life. You check her wardrobe and drawers. She's taken nearly all her clothes – smarter, more expensive than yours – and her nicest underwear and tights, but she's left both sets of pyjamas, which causes a fresh wave of bitterness. You hate to think of her sleeping naked with Dana. You fold the pyjamas anyway, and place them in a bag. You take down the white fairy lights she'd strung over the headboard and throw them on top of the pyjamas. In the bathroom cabinet, you find her pomegranate body butter (a birthday gift from your mother) and her shower cap. You pack those, and two of the expensive white bath sheets (the older ones) and a hand towel.

In the kitchen, you decide she can have the juicer, two white plates, two white cereal bowls, two white mugs and a fistful of cutlery. But not the stove-top percolator. Let her new, amazing woman make her coffee. You wrap them all in the oldest tea towels and put them in a separate bag.

So that just leaves the living room. From the bookshelves, you take down and pack her novels, and books on Eastern philosophy and popular psychology. The furniture came with the flat, but together you'd bought a grey, lambswool blanket and matching cushions for the sofa. Sometimes, in the past, you and Emily made love on that sofa, her head resting on one of those cushions, and you would wrap her, afterwards, in the blanket. Will Dana be making love to Emily right now? You feel bile burn your oesophagus. You decide they can have the cushions and blankets, all of which, when you hold them to your face, smell faintly of Emily's vanilla scented shampoo. You hope they'll feel so guilty they'll have to get rid of them. You stuff them into the bag.

To the right of the chimney breast there's a small, built-in cupboard. The glory hole, Emily called it. Inside, it smells musty. You find a bag of obsolete phone chargers, their wires tangled, and a box containing her lava lamp.

She bought it six years ago, at the end of a day trip to Brighton, shortly after you both left the beach on your way back to the station – scurrying into a shop full of touristy tat because, suddenly, there was a thunderstorm with heavy rain, and neither of you had an umbrella. You'd both been drinking wine all afternoon, and were giggling, whispering, trying to decide how long you could take shelter in this busy, over-stuffed shop. You were considering buying each other mugs with comic messages – *Galley Slave* and *You Don't Have to Be Mad to Work Here But It Helps!* – when Emily spotted a shelf of boxed lava lamps. The one at the end was set up and working. Lurid blue globules of wax were rising and falling through green liquid.

'Look, isn't that the most gorgeous thing *ever*?' she shrieked. 'Those blobs … they're like … they're squashy tomatoes, blood platelets…'

'They're blue,' you pointed out. 'Tomatoes and platelets are red.'

She rolled her eyes, took a box off the shelf and marched up to the counter. On the train, she cradled it on her lap. Back at the flat, she placed the lava lamp on the coffee table, plugged it in and insisted you sat and watched together, whilst it heated up, to see 'all the little miracles'. The one she'd bought had orangey-red wax and sky-blue liquid and a lightweight silver-coloured base. You thought it looked silly and kitsch, out of place in a room full of muted colours.

'Look,' she said, snuggling up to you. 'Can't you *see*? They're little *creatures*. They can be our pretend pets.' She laughed, and leaned forward, pointing. 'Better than pets – they won't need any maintenance. Actually, forget pets. *Look!* A headless buddha, bumping into a detached placenta. That big one, there … that's a spacehopper. Don't you just *love* them?'

You didn't. You saw heated globules of wax squeezing themselves up from the base and rising to the top of the lamp, and hanging around for a few minutes, before falling down to the base, occasionally colliding with another lump of molten wax. You explained the science to Emily, telling her liquid and wax are different densities, so they can never dissolve or blend. As the wax blobs heat, their molecules move further apart, they become lighter, they rise. And when they reach the top, they cool, and their molecules move closer together, so they become denser, and fall.

But she wasn't listening. She told you she thought the globules were a metaphor for the life cycle and reincarnation. Everything was impermanent, everything that seemed to be solid will fall apart, re-form, appear again. To humour her, you tried to look as though you'd received an amazing epiphany, and nodded.

Now, you unravel the flex and plug it into a power socket. The light pings on immediately, but nothing happens for several minutes, as the wax heats. Then slowly an orange-red globule squeezes itself into a spherical shape and begins to stretch upwards, followed thirty seconds later by another globule. The molecules are moving further apart. You remember Emily's enraptured whisper, the warmth of her head on your chest as you stroked her hair. 'They're singing to each other, can you hear them, Kirsty? Little ghosts. They're singing laments.'

She grew bored with it, though, after a few weeks, decided it was a tacky impulse buy. You came home from a year seven parents' evening to find it gone. You assumed at the time she'd given it to a charity shop.

Outside, it's already dark. You draw the curtains and turn on the spotlights, clipped to the bookshelves. The lava lamp looks less garish, now there's more light. You retrieve the blanket and cushions from the bag and curl up on the sofa, with the blanket over you and a cushion under your head.

An hour later, you wake slowly, stretch, and watch the lamp glowing, the wax blobs rising and falling. You sit up properly and try to see what Emily saw. The blobs representing something beyond themselves. After a few minutes, concentrating hard, you identify helium balloons, but this feels unsatisfying. Not original enough. You borrow Emily's images. Spacehoppers, yes. Headless buddhas, yes. Detached placentas, no.

Then suddenly, you see them. Jellyfish. The way they drift upwards. How they pulse and flex. Jellyfish! You lean forward and brush the sides of their red-hot glass with your fingertips.

You fetch the Merlot and a glass from the kitchen and drink rapidly, staring at the lamp. Your attention is riveted by what you now see as a whole bloom of small, trapped jellyfish, rising and falling. You remember the first time you saw a single jellyfish pulse upwards in its huge tank – you must have been nine or ten – in a dank-smelling, echoey Sea Life Centre. From the phylum Cnidaria; their bell shape pulsates to provide propulsion and locomotion. Jellyfish have no eyes, noses, brains or hearts. They can live for a few hours, or a few years. In some species, their stings can be lethal.

You jump, spilling wine down your jumper, as you hear a key scraping in the lock, the front door opening. You hear the front door click shut. Then the living room door opens. Emily wears a short, white raincoat you don't recognise, and her wavy hair is tousled and damp. She looks fresh and pretty. Younger. She smells nice, too – some grapefruit-scented body lotion or spray.

She stares at the lava lamp, and passes a hand through her hair. 'Oh my God, that thing! It still works?'

'Of course.'

'Wow. I'd forgotten all about it.'

You stand up, take her hands and pull her into the room. Her fingers are cool. She doesn't meet your eyes.

'Remember you said they were squashy tomatoes, or platelets?' She frowns. 'Then you said headless buddhas. You did! Headless buddhas bumping into detached placentas—'

She pulls away and folds her arms. You so badly want to hold her close, kiss her. 'Ugh, placentas, really? I was probably pissed—'

'But I've worked it out. They're jellyfish, trapped jellyfish.'

She laughs uncomfortably. 'No, wrong shape. And they'd have those, those trailing things if—'

'You're being too literal. You have to really *look*.' You sit on the sofa and pull her down next to you. '*Really* look, and then you'll see what I can see.'

You both sit for a few minutes, the jellyfish rising and falling, rising and falling. She says nothing, though occasionally she clears her throat, in that delicate, almost silent way of hers. You sense how much she wants to leave. How she'll be thinking about the taxi outside. And Dana. Maybe, under the white raincoat, under her clothes, she's wearing expensive, lacy underwear Dana's bought her.

You try to stop your voice from shaking. 'Can I keep them?'

'Them?'

'The jellyfish. You don't want them?'

'No, no. You keep it.'

'*Them*.'

She stands up, hands you her keys. 'Kirsty,' she says gently, kissing the top of your head – a sharp waft of grapefruit – 'be happy.'

You hear rustling as she gathers up the bags in the hallway, hear the front door bang and an engine start. You sit alone with the jellyfish, trapped in their glass tank, watching them rise and fall, rise and fall. You lean towards them, close your eyes, certain you can hear a faint, low-frequency hum. Maybe the lamp's electricity?

But then you hear *them*, really hear them. They're not silent. And they're not singing laments, or anything else. They're sniggering as they collide, they're colluding, whispering about how they will each sting somebody to death.

Catherine Smith lives in East Sussex and is a published and anthologised writer of fiction and poetry, some of which has been adapted for Live Literature performances. Two of her full-length poetry collections have been shortlisted for Forward Prizes. She is also a self-employed poetry and fiction tutor and mentor, who works with writing organisations including New Writing South and the Arvon Foundation. She buys the BSSA anthology every year but this is her first entry, and she is absolutely delighted to be a contributor.

Joshua Levy

Pigeons

Well, the pigeons ate the wedding rice and exploded somewhere over San Antonio.

I picked up the newlyweds and asked them where they wanted to go. They said, 'We don't care, we don't know, anywhere, just go.'

'I can do that,' I said.

I piloted the limousine out of the parking lot and past rows of painted wooden houses clinging to the sides of the road. We were thirty miles from Mexico. They had tied the knot in Brackettville – at that phony Alamo. The bride winked in my rear-view mirror while her husband nibbled gleefully on her earlobe. Her hair was auburn, her skin the colour of finely stirred chocolate milk – just a real good-looking girl in a tight, white wedding dress. Meanwhile, the groom was taller and blonder and more muscular than I could ever be. Neither of them was wearing a mask, but I wasn't either, so I wasn't going to bring it up.

The newlyweds were laughing about some uncle named Jack who'd gotten too drunk and cried during his toast.

'What a doofus,' they said. 'But, also, like, what a total sweetheart!?'

As I drove, brief scenes played out in the windows of the houses. A man spooning soup; two women laughing hysterically in matching armchairs; a baby hoisted towards the ceiling by – well, probably the father.

The next time I looked in the rear-view mirror, things had evolved. The bride was straddling the groom and rocking back and forth on his lap. So, I raised the privacy divider and counted mailboxes zooming by.

Soon the road thickened into a country highway and yellow dashed lines broke out in the pavement like a rash. I drove between two lanes and imagined that my limousine was a giant zipper, and my job was to zip up all the dashed lines on the highway. In this way, I might heal America – which, lately, had been coming apart at the seams.

Lonely, I lowered the privacy divider: hoping to catch love in action. 'Care for some gum?'

The newlyweds were still in their clothes, but their bodies had become so entwined that they responded as if a single living creature.

'Huh?' they said. 'Oh, yeah, okay, sure.'

I pawed inside the glove compartment, fingers travelling over crumpled maps, binders, an empty protein bar wrapper. The gum was buried under my handgun.

'Bombs away!' I hollered.

The gum thumped the groom on the bridge of his nose. He yelped like a dog, and we all laughed.

Ever since I'd gotten married, I'd started working weddings, graduations and funerals. Eventually, the events bleed into each other and you begin to recognise the same recycled faces in the different parties.

I drove up a dusty hill dotted with prickly pear cactus and animal carcasses, while the newlyweds focused on each other's bodies. On the radio, a lawyer wanted to know if I'd recently been injured in a car accident. I hadn't, so I changed stations until Dolly Parton was singing a sad-ass song. I kept my eyes on the road. Dolly turned into Johnny, turned into Bonnie, turned into John Prine, turned into Hank Jr.

Outside of Concan, the groom noticed my gold wedding band.

'You got any advice for us, old man?'

Well, I thought for a mile. Finally, I said, 'Take pains to chew your food.'

The groom snorted. 'That's deep.'

'Any more pearls of wisdom?' asked the bride.

I wiped at a smudge on the windshield, but it turned out to be on the outside of the car, so I stopped doing that. I said, 'Make babies. That's your glue on days you can't stand each other. Babies are Crazy Glue when a marriage gets a crack in it.' I laughed, but they didn't, so I added, 'Don't you want babies?'

The bride said, 'Oh, yes!' The groom kind of nodded.

'One plus one equals three with a baby. That's romantic arithmetic,' I said, and I scratched at my nose until a flake of dead skin detached. Then I rolled it into a ball and launched it into the universe.

After I'd said my piece, we drove on in silence. How my words had gone over, I couldn't tell. Potent advice or preachy as hell?

My wife and I didn't have any children. We tried, we couldn't. For years it was all we talked about and then we weren't even able to do that. It had been about a month since I'd spoken with my wife at all. The last time was in the kitchen, when out of the blue, she said, 'I blame the end of our marriage on you not lifting a finger when I choked on those Cheetos.'

I put my fork down on my plate. I was almost done eating, anyways.

'What?'

'Oh, there are other reasons,' she continued. 'Your passive-aggressive jokes about my weight, the socks on the floor, and all the white lies we've fed each other. But – and here's where I want to be honest – that time I choked on a Cheeto and you didn't even ask if I was okay? I just can't forgive you for that.'

'What the fuck are you talking about?'

'Karen says I deserve "a man of action". Like Eric. She's always comparing you to Eric. Last week, Eric beat up a teenager who was stealing Amazon packages from their front porch.'

'You want me to beat up a teenager?'

'What I'm trying to say is that I want a divorce, honey.'

'Is this the menopause talking?'

'Don't you even!' she said.

'I'm serious,' I said, because I'm an idiot. 'What's this about Cheetos? I don't know anything about Cheetos. Do you want to hear what I think? I think you're thinking of someone else, that's what I think.'

She stood out of her chair faster than I'd ever seen her move before and walked straight out of the kitchen.

'Where did you store our luggage!?' She practically screamed it down the hall.

I went to the liquor cabinet and poured us drinks but drank them both while I listened to drawers slamming in our bedroom.

Somewhere in Concan, we passed a playground. The newlyweds shouted, 'Hey! Please! Stop!' So, I stopped.

The pair spilled out and raced towards a swing-set. The bride barefoot, the groom hot in pursuit. I pulled an insulated thermos out of a bag on the passenger seat and took a satisfying swig. The thermos was filled with whiskey and a few drowned ice cubes.

Through the windshield, I watched the groom hoist the bride onto a swing and shove her closer and closer to the sun. Children ran in a sloppy circle around the swing set, kicking up sand. They looked like tiny ninjas behind their Covid masks.

Suddenly, the bride launched herself off the swing and hung in the breeze for a perfect second before gravity got its hooks in her and dragged her back down. She landed on her feet and they both scurried over to a slide.

These two will be a while, I thought, climbing out of the limousine.

I meandered through the park. It was humid outside. I felt my chest hairs stick to my dress shirt almost immediately.

At the other end of the park was a cemetery. I approached one of the headstones. In dainty calligraphy, the inscription read:

Christine McCray: 1942 – 2017
James McCray: 1939 –

I placed a finger on the smooth, unblemished spot of the slab of stone where James's date of death would be added when he died, and I tried to guess the date.

'I hope you get to see your wife soon,' I whispered.

The stone was warm. On the left-hand side of the grave, in front of the headstone, was a flowerbed with purple flowers and a plaque with the word 'Christine'. To the right of this was only grass, for now. I wondered how couples decide who goes where in the ground. I'd want my usual side of the bed.

I still loved my wife. I told her I loved her almost every day we were together, for over thirty years. Christ, I even loved waking up early on the weekends just to watch her sleep. She had this way of turning on her side and spooning her pillow and scrunching her toes and poking them out of the sheets that killed me. Once upon a time she used to love me too. Somehow, when I wasn't paying attention, her love must have faded like a suntan, until one day it had gone.

I guess I don't understand love as well as I thought I did. Last week, before working a wedding, I drove to the library for the first time in decades and asked the librarian if she had any books to fix a broken relationship. I was out of ideas by then. The librarian recommended the book *Loving for Dummies*. She said I'd find it in the Social Sciences aisle. I read the first twenty pages sitting on a faded library armchair by the gender-neutral bathroom. The author kept talking about how love is a verb, how love isn't something you say, it's something you do. I wish they taught things like that in school.

I lifted my thermos to my lips, but it was empty.

When I got back to the limousine, the newlyweds were nowhere in sight. They weren't in the playground – which had grown a new crop of children and parents, and they weren't inside the limo – which I had accidently left unlocked. I climbed messily inside the driver's seat and closed my eyes. But I couldn't stop picturing my wife's face, so I opened my eyes again. A few seconds later, when they closed again, all I could see were shades of black.

I woke to banging on my window. The groom was holding a greasy paper bag up for me to see. The bride raised her empty hands to her mouth and pretended to take a giant bite out of something delicious.

'Thanks for waiting,' the groom said, sliding in. 'We got crazy hungry.'

'What's next for you two?' I said.

'Like, now that we're married?' the bride asked.

'Where should I drop you off?'

'Oh! Ha!' the bride said.

The groom crammed a fat French fry into his mouth. 'Our waitress recommended a cool hotel, but I don't remember the name. It starts with an F.'

'The Frio Country Resort,' the bride said.

'I know it well,' I said, and started to drive.

The bride said, 'I told you I'm good with names, baby.'

'Baby, you're fucking amazing, and that's exactly why I married you.'

'Let's get married again tomorrow,' she said.

'What's next for you two, anyways?' I asked. 'You've got me curious.'

'Huh?' they said.

'Now that you're married.'

'Like, our hopes and dreams and etcetera?' she said, tipping her head to the side.

'Bingo.'

'We have big dreams,' the groom said.

'The biggest,' added the bride. 'Huge!'

But I didn't hear them after that. I was daydreaming about my own bride. On our honeymoon, naked in bed, my wife had torn a sheet of paper from the hotel stationery and we'd written a list of the things we were excited to do together. We wrote: 'visit the pyramids', because a travelling mummy exhibition had been our first date, and we wrote: 'get good at tennis', because tennis seemed like something we could do together, and we wrote: 'grow a family'.

I remember a lot of dreams that didn't happen.

'Wait! Snacks for the hotel!' they yelled.

We had passed a 7-Eleven.

I made a sharp U-turn and parked facing the gas station. Arms linked, the newlyweds went inside.

I felt sad and congested. I opened the glove compartment and found a crumpled tissue. I blew my nose one nostril at a time. Then I removed the handgun and placed it on my lap. It had been a Christmas gift from my wife. I was pretty sure it was loaded. I stared at the gun.

Finally, the newlyweds came out of the 7- Eleven. Their faces were bright and vivid in the sunlight. The groom was gripping a bottle of wine and the bride had a humongous bag of chips tucked under her arm. They were holding hands. Jesus Christ, they looked happy.

The bride let go of the groom's hand to reach inside the bag of chips. They were framed in the centre of my windshield, like I was watching a drive-in movie. The groom said something, and the bride burst out laughing. She pointed to her throat. She kept pointing to her throat.

Something wasn't right. I flung open the car door, and I ran.

'I see you!' I yelled. 'I see you! I see you!!'

I ran behind her and stuck out my leg and clasped my hand around my fist and thrust it into her stomach until the groom yanked me off her and she gasped and began to cough.

Everything seemed out of focus. I rubbed my eyes with my sleeve, but the bride still looked blurry. She could have been any bride.

'What the hell!' the groom shouted. 'Why did you do that?'

My hands were trembling. I rubbed my eyes again, and when I turned my hands back over, they were wet.

The groom slapped me hard on the back. 'Whatever, man,' he said. 'It's all good.'

The bride scowled at me. I bent down and slowly, carefully, picked up the bag of chips and handed it to her. But she wasn't holding it properly, and a few chips spilled out. The groom kissed the top of the bride's head and she looked up at him and smiled. A few more chips spilled out. The newlyweds started walking towards the limousine. A white pigeon loitering by the car lifted into the air. As it flapped away, I remembered reading somewhere that pigeons mate for life.

I was still thinking about that when I drove home.

Joshua Levy writes in many genres and was last year's Canadian Broadcasting Corporation (CBC) Writer-In-Residence. His work has been published by Oxford University Press, Vehicle Press and Mansfield Press, and has appeared in literary journals such as *Maisonneuve, Malahat Review* and *The Rumpus*. Levy is a recent winner of the CNFC/Carte Blanche Nonfiction Prize, Prairie Fire Nonfiction Prize, SLS Nonfiction Prize and CBC/QWF Fiction Prize. His first book of poetry, *The Loudest Thing*, was published in 2019, and he is currently working on a novel. Levy lives in Montreal with his wife.

Samanthi Munasing

Two Samosas and a Bag of Crisps

She practised moves, watched by the silvery sliver of moon outside the window. Pull the right hand back, make into fist, jab, jab, jab. Utter the words, 'F**k you,' without a quiver in the voice. The eyes in the mirror stared back, unconvinced. Still.

'Farah! You be late!' Uma, hissing so as not to wake the baby. Farah adjusted the hijab, pulled the tights out from the crotch area – she needed a bigger size – grabbed the school bag, and headed down the stairs. In the kitchen, Uma waited, holding a glass of milk. Why does she have to act like the Queen presenting a trophy every morning? Just leave it on the table, Ma! Farah sat down.

'Tost?' Uma rearranged the shawl around her head and placed the glass on the table.

'No, cereal.'

Across the road, Mr Sayyid wheeled his bike, on his way to work. The bare branches in the ash tree stretched towards the grey sky, searching for the sun. Uma poured Sugar Puffs into the bowl on the table and opened the fridge. She hated throwing food away – a spoonful of potato curry in foil, half a boiled carrot for the baby, a ball of dough wrapped in cling film or kitchen paper – all sheltered in the fridge until eaten, or being tossed in the bin. Afterwards, she always prayed for forgiveness at the waste. Now she pulled out the plastic lunch box and placed it in Farah's backpack. The baby began his mewl, and Uma hurried out, calling, 'Finish milk.' Ma had looked tired, she managed little sleep – what with the baby and the dawn prayers – after which she often just padded around the house like some phantom, until breakfast.

'Habibi,' Uma cooed in the living room. 'Bibi...ee.'

Grabbing a fistful of cereal, Farah darted out the back door before Uma returned with the baby. When would she start buying semi-skimmed? Couldn't Uma see how fat they were both getting?

Janine's immaculate nails – the colour of boiled salmon – spread out as Farah tried to pass her.

'In there.' Farah was shoved into the locker room. The door clicked shut. Elsabeth (no I, no Z), examined her face in a small mirror by the window. Tanisha was doubled up, holding onto skinny ribs, braids swaying, laughing at some joke Farah had missed. She was in the Clone Zone – short skirts, long legs, pale pink hair clips, identical Rhianna bags.

'Morning, freak,' Tanisha called as Janine pulled at the hijab. Secured with discreet safety pins, it wasn't going to budge. Ha, ha! Janine's face loomed close. A smattering of freckles, like lentils around a thin, pointed nose. 'Get this disgusting thing off!' she yapped, chewing. She smelled of Diet Coke and gum. The Clones never consumed anything else. Maybe the occasional packet of crisps. That's why they were whippet thin compared to Farah. She'd be watching her diet from now on. And this time she'd stick to it.

It was Tanisha's turn with the hijab. Farah lowered her head, trapping the front of the scarf between neck and chin. A vicious shove from behind, and she bumped right into those braids and fell, as Tanisha stepped back. If only she had pulled at those dangling ropes. Two girls came into the locker room. Year seven.

'Out,' Janine barked. The girls left. Tanisha grabbed the backpack. She took out the lunch box and threw it at Janine, who caught it deftly and prised it open. She picked out a samosa between thumb and forefinger and brought it up to her small, delicate nose, pinkly glowing.

'Yuck.' She frowned. 'This is rank! Smell it!' She turned towards Elsabeth, now applying mascara.

'No, no. I got Revolution on.' Elsabeth put her hand up. The mirror glinted, star-like, catching a truant ray of sun. Tanisha tossed things out of Farah's bag with a theatrical swirl. Notebook, text books, French dictionary. The second bell screeched just as she opened the pencil box and scattered the two Biros, pencils and rubbers onto the floor. Sound of scurrying feet in the corridor. Elsabeth placed the mirror and mascara in her bag.

'Wanna go into town on Saturday?' she asked Tanisha. The door opened and Mrs Fox peered in.

'Girls! Didn't you hear the bell? Come on! Farah, on your feet!' Janine shed the contents of the lunch box on the floor – two samosas and a bag of crisps.

'Coming, miss,' she said, picking up her bag. Elsabeth walked languidly to the door, stepping carefully on the food. They went out.

'Get a move on, Farah,' Mrs Fox called again before the door shut behind her. Farah collected the broken bits of food and put them back in the lunch box.

Annie plonked down at the desk next to Farah. Catherine rushed in to sit a few desks away, between Jill and Kamara. Lucky them. It would be so nice to sit next to Catherine. Slim as a tulip stalk, golden hair framing a tranquil face. So cool.

Catherine Watching: cleaning a paint brush with a careful, mysterious delicacy, a flash of a smile when Mrs Catt read out Farah's poem. Everyone wanted to be Catherine's friend. Only *she* didn't seem to care, always alone, occasionally with Sophie, who had nothing going for *her*. Catherine was usually the last to get to class; there was no chance to sit next to her, really.

She had joined the school last spring and was good at English – although not as good as Farah – and better at art. Despite being in the same class, they hardly spoke. Annie said that Catherine's father had lost his job and she'd had to leave St Bede's, the private school in Denton. Annie made things up, but there was definitely a sort of sadness in Catherine. One day, she'd be a friend. That time last summer gave Farah hope.

A week before breaking up, most pupils had lunch on the grassy bank outside the canteen. Farah had her copy of *Glamour* open, but she was acutely aware of Catherine close by, her face lifted to the sun, eyes shut. She was conscious, too, of the Clones – further away – their laughter drifting downwind at regular intervals. A well-honed sixth sense always at the ready, Janine's sudden dash was a warning, but it took only a few seconds. The thud of Janine's trainer on her back was more humiliating than painful. Through the hot fog of shame, she heard Catherine.

'Get lost Janine,' she said, her voice loud and clear. 'Why don't you mind your own business?' For a moment they glared at each other, before Janine pranced off without a word.

'Thanks', Farah tried to say, but before she could unglue the words, Catherine was up and sauntering towards the canteen without ever looking her way. Later, she wondered how Catherine knew. After all, her eyes had been closed. Maybe they had a sort of *connection*.

A cold breeze chased a coppery leaf across the field. Away from the main school building, behind the Portacabins used as changing rooms, she felt safe. On a cold day like this, the Clones wouldn't venture this way. In fact, nobody should, it was about to rain. Wrong! Annie came waddling around the corner.

'There you are!' she said cheerfully, waving a carton of Ribena. 'Brrr … nippy.' Farah smiled weakly, tugging at the hood on her anorak. Annie slid on to the moist bench, sucking noisily. Squeak, squeak.

They watched the grass, lush with rain, the moody sky. The empty carton sailed towards the open rubbish can and fell on a clump of soggy weeds.

'You missed.'

'Yah.' Annie smiled, producing a Mars bar.

'Want some?'

'Nah, ta.' Farah stood up. Maybe try one of the music rooms.

'Heard you … uh … lost your lunch.' Annie began to unwrap the chocolate carefully. She inspected the exposed square for a moment before biting into it with a faint, crunching noise. Drops of rain began to fall, icy, sharp.

'I used to get stuff from that lot,' she continued. 'But I whupped Janine with my bag once. She had a right bruiser. Leaves me alone now.' Before each bite, Annie pulled off just the right amount of wrapper. Hunger made Farah dizzy. Or was it knowing that everyone – including Catherine – must know of her shame? Even Annie had the guts to face up to Janine. Even she. 'Gotta go,' Farah muttered, and scurried off, biting her lip to prevent anything silly happening.

Mr Fulsome droned on. Electricity, grounding. Perhaps she should ask a question – just to please him. No one else ever did. But an image of malfunctioning hair straighteners flashed across her mind. Blond hair and braids shrivelling like burning paper. Her stomach purred happily. Jason Fielding put his hand up. Mr Fulsome nodded.

'Sir…,' Jason said. 'Cow getting laid in here.' Everyone laughed. Catherine too, probably. F**k Jason. Farah placed her hands on her burning cheeks. Jason swaggered out.

Later, she watched from the music room on the second floor: the mad rush, voices calling, car horns squeaking. Once or twice, in the swiftly fading light, she thought she saw a flash of pink. Last week they had waited by the Common with Jason and Alan. The sound of their laughter still echoed in her ears.

Next time, she'd be ready. '*The world is a dangerous place. Not because of those who do evil, but because of those who look on and do nothing*.' Einstein, her hero.

She took the longer route home, hurrying all the way – Uma watched the clock like a hawk. Sure enough, the moment Farah sneaked in the door, Uma appeared, clutching the small knife she used to gut fish. The smell of hot oil was thick in the air.

'You late,' Uma whispered, 'Change. Appa ready. Five minutes.' She returned to the smoky kitchen. Uma was learning English and didn't use prepositions yet. In the bedroom, Farah took off her headscarf, changed into a tracksuit bottom and T-shirt, and sped down the stairs. She was starving. There was mackerel fried in a spicy batter, rice and okra for dinner.

'You're hungry!' Appa smiled gently.

'Um… Netball practice.' There was no point in sharing her shame.

Appa asked the question he asked every day.

'What did you learn today?'

It pleased him, to 'take her lessons'. He had taught mathematics in his village school in Afghanistan. But the modern approach to maths irritated him. So, really, he was very little help. Later, she cleared the table, finished homework and prepared for next day's lessons. She watched the news. Knives in schools.

Appa pulled open the curtains. A whiff of last night's fried fish escaped the forest of his beard as he kissed Farah. 'M awake, Pa,' she muttered, eyes firmly closed. A moment later, she heard him leave. Appa always had some smell about him: fish, lemons, curry, even bread. Working as a delivery man for an Indian grocer during the day, and at the Curry King in the evenings, he smelled of whatever he'd last delivered. She didn't know what his true smell was. Everyone had one; Janine said she could smell Farah from the other end of the corridor. When she was little, Appa would speak of the spring fragrance back home. How he sat for hours in his small orchard, watching the blossoming fruit trees tremble in the breeze. That was before the Taliban came down from the mountains. Farah imagined Appa's true smell had the scent of apple blossom and green rivers full of melting snow. But he smelled nothing like that really.

Rain sputtered against the window. The high-pitched whining of the baby drilled through the thin walls. Annie. What was the point in thinking of all that? Rolling out of bed, Farah stepped over to the mirror.

In the ashy, morning light, the black shadows below puffy eyes made her look like a brown panda. Turning away, she pulled out a notebook from under the bed. A diary of sorts, full of scribbled phrases, verses, tear-soaked thoughts. '*Cowards die many times before their deaths; the valiant never taste death but once*.' '*Boldness, be my friend*.' Trembling, she replaced the book. She was brave. She was clever.

The knife was in the school bag – where she had placed it last night – and still smelled faintly fishy.

Before the mirror, she held it close to her side. 'One, two, three,' she whispered, and lunging forward, thrust the knife towards her own image, connecting a few inches above the navel, in that flabby pocket of flesh. Maybe the arm was easier. Again, 'One, two…'

And again. Not too hard. Just a scratch should do.

The clouds raced across the sky as if late for a heavenly appointment as Farah left the house. 'One, two,' she counted in her head. Her fingers touched the cold blade in her pocket. Einstein and Shakespeare would guide her today.

Samanthi Munasing was born in Sri Lanka and lives in Alfriston. She belongs to the Chalk Circle, a group of writers based in Sussex. An Anthology of their short stories will be launched in October. Her short story, 'Rice on a Banana Leaf', was placed third in the 2020 Bath Short Story Award. She is currently working on a novel.

James Young

At Anderson's Field

They parked their large, practical cars along the lanes and hurried, brows glistening, to the gates. Their differences set aside, they exchanged pleasantries as they waited – *isn't that a great day for it* and *sure they said it would rain but then you never can tell.* But as the sun climbed higher and the queue became longer, the chatter turned darker – *'Mon to bollix there, Billy!* and *how hard can it be to give a man his feckin' change?* The muttering grew louder – *suppose them 'uns will be let in first again*, someone shouted – the temperature crept towards twenty-two, and the jostling began, until soon the temporary fences were rocking back and forth on their supports. Finally, the order came crackling over the walkie-talkies of the security guards – *better let them in or we'll have a feckin' riot on our hands.* The gates swung open; the crowd pushed forward and with a long, yodelled *yeeeeoooo!* burst jubilantly into the country fair.

Should have set off half an hour ago, said Julie's father, his knuckles white on the steering wheel of their aging hatchback. Excited, love? her mother asked, leaning backwards from the passenger seat. No, said Julie, her arms folded tightly across her chest. There'll be no decent spaces, grumbled her father, we'll have to park miles away. You and your parking, Julie's mother sighed. She reached over and tuned the radio to a country station, as in the back Julie began to cry, her wailing keeping time with the warbling vocals of the music. For feck's sake, Julie's father said, that's all we need. I want John, Julie sobbed, fingering the yellow leather lead in her hand, I want him!

They unspooled through the stalls, the men mooning dreamily at the hay tedders, the dehorning boxes, the rapid empty drinkers; the women heading for the baking tent to catch a glimpse of the winner of the fruit tart competition, wondering was it too early for another cup of tea, or even (and God the *indulgence* of it) a 99. When the hands of the clock by the farming apparel stand struck noon, all of them began to drift, past the British blues and beef shorthorns with their queasy reek of shit, past the gleaming combine harvester, its tyres as big as boats, past the collection of antique chainsaws glittering in the sun, towards Anderson's Field. There, by the sign that read *Dog Show – 2 pm*, the crowd grew clotted, tempers began to fray, and oaths and expletives were uttered – *mind where yer feckin' goin'!* and *mind yerself, ye feckin' arse!* Soon, though, all found spots around the field, and their cries – of predictions and favourites (*my money's on young Peter from the meatpacking factory and wee Sheba for the collie class; Peter and Sheba yer backside, it's Big Joe from McCormack's and Daisy whose names are on the cup!*), of memories of champions past (*do you mind old Tom's Max back in '93, now thon was a pup and a half!*) – formed a constant ululation, drowning out the birds.

Told you we'd find a place, Julie's mother said, as Julie's father squeezed their car in beside a Land Rover on a verge not far from the gates. Can you not keep her quiet? he said, as Julie wept and beat her fists on her legs, leaving unhappy blotches on her skin. John can't even walk on a lead, love, said her mother gently, sure he almost choked himself last time you tried. But you said, sobbed Julie, thrusting her fist against her small white teeth. People say a lot of things, said her father. Maybe next year, love, said her mother. You said that last year, said Julie, her eyes marbled with tears. Mind you don't scratch this man's doors as you get out, said her father, clambering from the car, planting his large black boots on the soil. Look, said Julie's mother, waving at a thick-kneed woman teetering down the lane, there's Helen from Zumba!

At two on the dot, the Reverend, his bald head glinting brightly in the sun, emerged from the judges' tent. Testing, one two, testing, one two, he said into his mic, gazing at the roseate wall of faces surrounding the field, waiting for the chatter to subside, relishing the moment the way a cup final referee savours the final seconds before kick-off. Eventually, the silence was complete, but for one small bird singing in a nearby tree. Right folks, cried the Reverend, let's get this show on the road! The first dogs and their owners began to file out of the tent, and from the crowd rose up the rumble – *yeeeeoooo!*

We'll miss the collies if we don't hurry, Julie's father said as they passed through the gates, the cheers from Anderson's Field billowing around the now abandoned stalls. We could still go back for him, Julie sniffed, wiping her nose with one hand, John's bright yellow lead in the other. Will you not shut your hole about that feckin' dog, snapped her father. Tom, said Julie's mother, don't talk to her like that! Sorry love, said Julie's father, we'll get you a 99 instead, and he bent down and took her hand. No, shouted Julie, and, wriggling from his grasp, she ran off, pulling John's lead behind her. She ran past the hay tedders, the dehorning boxes, the rapid empty drinkers;

past the baking tent, the cattle sheds, the gleaming combine harvester; she ran past the antique chainsaws, glittering in the sun, until at last she reached Anderson's Field, where she burrowed into the hot, dank entanglement of legs and feet and bags and crotches and arses. She crawled and clambered amongst them for what seemed like hours, until finally she ducked under a rope and emerged from the gloom into a bright patch of sunlight on a large and open sea of grass.

Slurping on soft drinks and sucking slowly on boiled sweets, they watched, enraptured, as the dogs and their owners paraded around the field. They cheered the pampered Pekingese and clapped the thrusting spaniels; they whistled the stately wolfhounds and hurrahed the handsome huskies; they made such a din that no one heard the loudspeaker announcement of *a little girl has been lost, a little girl has been lost*. The mood remained peaceable right through the terriers and the toys, the sporting class and the hounds. Barley sugar? a woman in a deckchair said to her neighbour. Don't mind if I do, said the second woman, reaching over and taking a sweet, as a sturdy bulldog brought the utility group to a close. Looks like the big moment is finally here, said the first woman, holding out the bag in case her neighbour was partial to another, my money's on young Peter from the meatpacking factory and his wee Sheba. Dearie me, said the second woman, shaking her head, I fear you're in for a disappointment, it'll be Big Joe from McCormack's and Daisy's turn this time. Is that right? the first woman said coldly, withdrawing her bag of sweets. Right folks, cried the Reverend from the field, it's the one you've all been waiting for, and a man behind the women screamed, here they come, here they come! Then, as the air around the field seemed to tremble, the collies and their owners began to file out from the tent, led by Peter and Sheba, with Big Joe and Daisy not far behind. A chant sprung up – *Sheba! Sheba!* – followed quickly by another – *Daisy! Daisy!* – and suddenly arguments were breaking out all around the field. Look how glossy wee Sheba's coat is, yelled the woman with the sweets, she's the champion for sure! Never mind the barley sugars, cried the second woman, it's the wine gums you've been on, if you think that mangy beast can win! I'll give you wine gums, said the first woman, pulling back her arm as though to strike her neighbour, before they were interrupted by the man behind them. Would you two shut your feckin' holes, he said, look at this now! And he pointed, as many of the crowd were now pointing, at the little girl bringing up the rear of the parade.

Julie walked around the field, holding the yellow lead so that its stiff leather loop was suspended at just the height of a dog's neck, smiling shyly at the Reverend, the crowd and the other contestants, all of whom watched in silence. When she had completed her circuit she knelt down, patted the air, and whispered, there's a good boy, John, there's a good boy, just as the Reverend walked over. Hello, dear, he said, scratching at a troubling itch that had appeared behind his ear. Hello, Reverend, said Julie. Is this your dog? asked the Reverend, crouching down. Yes, Reverend, said Julie. And what's his name? asked the Reverend. John, said Julie. Is that right now? said the Reverend, well, John's a great name for a dog. Thank you, Reverend, said Julie. Now, dear, said the Reverend, getting to his feet and putting his hands on his hips, you do know this is a very important dog show, don't you? It's not for playing, or pretending. But I'm not playing or pretending, Reverend, said Julie. I know, dear, but you have to admit that John here, well, said the Reverend, before realising he didn't quite know how to finish his sentence.

Later, when they talk about it in the pubs, and in the car park after church, at the bingo and in the queue at the post office, no one will be able to remember from where the first shout came. Some will say it was a man near the judges' tent, who yelled *give her ten out of ten, Reverend!* Others will claim it was a woman near the big sign, who cried *sure that's a beautiful dog altogether!* What everyone will agree on is that soon the air was thick and heavy with raised, belligerent voices. *John's the winner for sure!* roared some, while *catch yourself on, ye bunch of feckin' eejits, there's no dog there at all!* bawled others. Opinion, it was noted afterwards, was divided along familiar lines, as though the arguments were seasoned by resentments hidden but not forgotten – ancient and tribal, as inevitable as blood. Forget Peter from the meatpacking factory, shouted the woman with the barley sugars, look at wee John's soft glossy coat and adorable white paws! Feck me, bellowed the second woman, I always knew you lot were a few sandwiches short of a picnic, but I'd no idea it was this bad. Are you saying I'm making that lovely wee animal up, ye blind hoor? screamed the first woman. What did you call me, ye silly bitch? yelled the second woman, grabbing the first woman's hair and yanking it from her scalp. Feck away off, shrieked the first woman, scraping her long painted fingernails across the other woman's cheek, drawing blood. Soon the scene was being repeated all around the field; punches were thrown, bottles were hurled and deckchairs were broken across backs, as neighbour turned upon neighbour, grabbing whatever weapons they could find.

There she is, shouted Julie's mother, there she is! Grabbing her husband by the hand, she ran out onto the field, past where the two women were grappling on the ground, past where a man was beating the Reverend with a fencepole, past where the winner of the fruit tart competition had just broken a beer bottle over the head of a security guard. Run! shouted Julie's mother, spotting, too late, the man walking towards their daughter, carrying a large glittering object. As she watched, he stopped, unleashed a fearsome, wordless cry, and pulled the ripcord on the antique chainsaw in his hands, before swinging it in a high, jewelled arc, until it met the shiny coat and soft flesh of the neck of the dog nearest to him, lopping off its head as though it was the top of an egg, the blood overrunning the sides like yolk, the head bouncing away, tongue lolling, across the grass, the little girl crouching beside it, screaming John, John! The man sank to his knees, letting the engine of the chainsaw idle and die, as all around the fighting stopped and the voices fell silent. For a long moment the only sound was that of a single bird singing in a tree, the occasional nervous cough, and little Julie's sobbing. Then, slowly shaking their heads and blinking, as though waking from a dream of bright and vivid colours, the crowd began to slowly drift away from Anderson's Field, to head back to where they had parked their cars. It was only later, when they had left the country fair behind, that they were able to speak of the things they had seen – *something has to be done*, they all agreed, *sure we can't have this kind of carry on every year*.

JAMES YOUNG is a writer and translator from Belfast. His short fiction has been published by *Wasafiri, Short Fiction Journal, Honest Ulsterman, HCE Review* and others, and he was shortlisted for the 2019 Wasafiri and 2020 Fish prizes. He is an editor at the *Short Fiction Journal* and is currently completing an MA in creative writing at Birkbeck.

Elizabeth Cooke

L'Chaim

Inside the CT scanner, her brain was throwing lightning bolts of Singing-in-the-Rain songs. *The angels must have sent you*, said Gene Kelly. *You were meant for me*.

'Something isn't quite right,' the German doctor told them.

'No kidding,' her husband muttered.

'Your wife has meningitis.'

Outside, a giant beech tree swayed in the wind. She lay perfectly still, faintly amused, certainly lost, while the parameters of the world sprang in and out, rubber walls and floors, flowers rapidly dying, the taste of herring, the clap of shoes in the corridor like rounds of applause.

The doctor was gone.

Her husband's face loomed into view. 'Does it hurt?'

She saw the words 'like an iron clamp on my brain' go skipping past, children out for a spree, consonants crowding on a playground slide, vowels on a violent red-painted swing, having a fine time out of control, out of reach of her mouth.

'If they ask me to turn off the machines, what shall I say?' he asked. She watched him leave, Mr Cool in his sharp suit, wishing like never before that someone would go after him with an axe.

They had come to Berlin for the weekend to mend their marriage.

It was before the Wall came down. On their first night in the city, their driver George had given them a whistle-stop tour of the city in his green Mercedes. He was in his early fifties, but seemed old. They went along Kurfurstendamm and her husband asked about the girls standing in line. 'The most expensive girls in the city,' George told them, as if they might want to hang out the window and ask the price. One of the girls had two Dobermann dogs on black leather leashes, and it had made her think of a dog that her parents used to have called Sally.

Perhaps the illness began then, producing a strange imagining of walking Sally down to the Kaiser Wilhelm church, seeing the world through an out-of-body kaleidoscope that mixed the warm evening with memory.

They had reached the church, and 'Firebombed on 22nd November 1943,' George had told them in a non-committal voice, as they looked up at the shattered church spire. He pronounced it 'bomb-bed', and showed them inside: the blue stained glass behind Christ the Redeemer. A girl sitting halfway along the aisle who wore a face like her own: comically tragic.

'How much is it?' her husband had asked.

'How much is what?' George asked.

'Those girls back there.' He meant it as a joke. He rolled his eyes and laughed.

George, glancing at her, smiled. Puzzled. 'You want this?'

'No,' she said. 'Being funny.'

'Ah, funny,' and George nodded. 'Very funny, yes.' But he looked at them both sadly, shrugging to himself. She noticed that his suit was very expensive, tailored to his thin body. In the car, sitting behind him in the back seat, she saw on the back of his neck a series of grid-like lines, and there was a round red mark offset to one side.

At a café they had lobster tail and prosecco.

The world began to whirl as they made their way to the hotel.

The next morning she had been taken to the hospital at dawn, her husband cursing all the way because she had had the audacity to fall down in an expensive hotel suite.

He always called her darling when he had something horrible to say. Like now.

'Darling, I have to go home.'

'Home?' And quite plainly she saw her mother standing beside him, dressed as she'd been that last day in the laughingly titled retirement home where her mother had decided to change the habits of a lifetime and become anything but retiring.

Her mother spoke up now. 'He's rubbish, that one. Going home indeed!'

'It's work,' he told her. 'I have so many meetings. I'll be back in ten days.'

Ten days. It meant nothing. Sometimes she would concentrate hard on the way that light crawled around the room, calculating that it was morning, and then, confusingly, they would bring in supper. She wanted to ask why the hours were all strung out and had sharp musical notes, and why the nurse smelled like sour violets. But nothing came out.

Before he left, she had heard him add to the doctor, 'She's always been a bit odd.'

'It is the illness,' the doctor replied. 'It is the Coxsackie B strain. It is viral. It is not oddness.'

Her husband had tapped the side of his head, then turned to wave at her. His hand went like this – in and out and in and out and in. His fingers were elongated tubes. She had closed her eyes.

One day she woke and found that she could sit up. They took her along to be washed, and the dirt sloughed off like peeling pith from an orange. They washed her hair and cleaned her teeth and they weighed her. She had lost twenty-one pounds in ten days and her arse was as flat as a board and she could count her ribs. When she said she was hungry at last, they brought her sauerkraut.

On the fourteenth day, George the driver came to see her.

He sat, embarrassed, by the side of her bed and explained that her husband still could not be there but that he was authorised to take her out in the car. He had brought a wheelchair and she wobbled into it.

'Where would you like to go?' he asked.

'The Wall,' she told him.

It was a cloudy day and they looked at the slogans painted on the even greyer slabs of the concrete. *Free the Baltic States*. In English. And paintings of broken hearts.

'It changes every day,' George said.

They went to the Reichstag and on the back steps in the fading light of day they looked over into the East. Beyond the wire there was a building and in the ground floor of the building there was a light and under the light a man was writing, head bowed in study. George pointed out the bullet holes in the walls above them.

She looked around her and realised that all the world was crazy.

'All the world is crazy,' she murmured. 'Not just me.'

'You are not crazy,' he said.

She looked at his worn face, his constantly weeping eyes, and the colour of the irises, almost white. He was only fifty-five or so but he was worn out with caring.

'In 1943, my father jumped out of a window,' he said. 'He landed in a pile of builder's sand and he buried himself in the sand. He lived like a dog for three years. Would that be crazy now?'

'Yes,' she said.

'Ah, but the times. Sometimes you must be crazy to save yourself,' he told her. 'Would you like to eat, or go back to the hospital?'

'The hospital,' she said. The irises had begun to merge into the white; he looked blind. Later, the red patch on his neck was livid in the fluorescence of the hospital lights and she dared to ask him what it was. 'Oh,' he whispered. 'I am touched by foolishness.'

'What kind of foolishness?'

'My mother tried to shoot me. There was not enough food for five.'

And he smiled benignly, as if – again – this was not foolishness but sense.

At the beginning of the third week, the doctor apologised for her long stay. 'We are a teaching hospital,' he told her. 'You are an interesting case.'

She thought of the early days lying there, unable even to reach the call for the nurse, and of students standing around her bed. One of them had oil underneath his fingernails. Or perhaps that had been her uncontrollable imagination, or the vivid and utterly three-dimensional dreams complete with taste and touch. Dreams that had slept at her side like lovers.

Dreams that had manufactured the dead and a vase of floating roses and so much more.

'Will I always have this alteration to my sight?'

'No. That will fade.'

'And walking in circles?' One of her legs – the right – wouldn't flex.

'No. It will improve.' He smiled at her. 'You are ready to be discharged. Is your husband coming to get you?'

She sent him a text but there was no reply. In sadness and desperation, she rang George, and he came and took her out to Charlottenburg, and to the museum where Nefertiti's face stared implacably into an ancient world that no one else could see. Inadvertently, in the museum lobby, she walked under a sacred gate that held curses for all who trespassed. George pointed it out to her with an apologetic air.

'I can't be cursed any more,' she told him. 'Look, I'm walking straight. I'm evidently invincible.'

It was November. They went down into the city, she holding George's arm. They went to see the Wall again, but there were crowds everywhere and the cold night pressed down on them all. A bright cloud of exhaled air hung over everyone in the lights from the border.

'Change,' George murmured.

He took her back down Kurfurstendamm. The girls had gone: even they were being drawn into the crowds. People streamed down the road towards the Brandenburg Gate.

They went into a café, and sat down by the window.

'What are you thinking?' she asked hm. 'Where are you in your head?'

'It is fifty-one years since Kristallnacht,' George said. 'I remember all the glass on the pavements. My father was taken away, and when he came back, we knew.' He glanced at her. 'And where are you?'

'I'm living in a small flat in the city. It's full of books,' she told him. 'I'll have Kaffee and Kuchen on a Sunday. I'll walk down Unter Den Linden in high heels. I will learn German. I will never go back home. I'll sing thanks for deliverance.'

'To do that here,' he murmured.

'If you can, I can,' she told him.

She asked for pickled fish, and it was brought with rye bread. They ate quietly and sat in the window and then somewhere around midnight, the Wall fell.

They remained where they were while all the world ran past with flowers towards the *Ossis*, the Easterners.

George lifted his drink. The schnapps flickered in the glass while sirens sounded and lights played across the table. 'A toast to chaos,' he said.

'L'chaim,' she responded. 'To life.'

Elizabeth Cooke is the author of fifteen novels and one non-fiction work. Living by the sea in Dorset, she has just finished a crime novel, and is researching an eighteenth-century biography. She has been writing since her first anthology of embarrassingly puppy-orientated poetry when she was six. Her story 'L'Chaim' sprang from some of her own experiences after contracting meningitis while on a weekend (unavoidably extended to a six-week) visit to Berlin in 1989. More about Elizabeth at her website elizabethcookeauthor.com.

Paul Bassett Davies

Your Car has Broken Down

My car has broken down, and you'll probably think I'm an idiot. Whatever's gone wrong, I hope it's not serious, but I hope it's serious enough to prove I'm not an idiot. I hope it's something I couldn't be expected to know about, or to have anticipated. Because not only has my car broken down, it's happened in the middle of nowhere, late at night.

Your car has broken down, and you're probably worried I'm going to think you're an idiot. That's quite common, as it happens. People feel guilty about calling a breakdown service, even though they're paying for it, and they can't be expected to know all about cars. Why should they? Having said that, I do come across some real idiots.

My car has broken down, and I'm glad you're here. You were pretty quick, given how remote this spot is. I was relieved when I saw your headlamps, winding across the moor towards me. I'm glad you've kept them on now you're here, and you're walking towards me holding some type of powerful work lamp on an extension lead.

Your car has broken down, and you're already telling me the tank is still half full, and you're assuring me you wouldn't be on this road if you'd thought the car was likely to break down. You seem like an intelligent person.

My car has broken down, and now you're checking the battery. Oh shit, please don't tell me the battery is flat. I'm very careful about that. Ok, now you're telling me the battery is fine. Thank god for that. You're fetching some type of device – whose name I've already forgotten – from your truck, so you can test the rest of the electrical system.

Your car has broken down, and if you're lucky I'll be able to fix it here and now, and you can be on your way again. To wherever you're going at this time of night on an isolated road across the moor. I can't deny I'm intrigued. You're in your late twenties or early thirties. Reasonably well-spoken, and clearly not local. You've got a London accent, although people like you always think everyone else has an accent except you. You probably think I've got a regional accent, and you probably think I'm working class. But I bet I earn more money than you, and my car – the car that's outside my house – is two years old, while that car of yours is well over ten years old, and it's a heap of shit. I wouldn't say that to your face. Unless I wanted to have a little game. We'll see.

My car has broken down, and you seem confident you can fix it. But maybe that's a professional tactic, so when it turns out you can't fix it, and I have to be towed to a garage, and spend money, I'll be convinced you did your best. For some reason, though, I get the feeling you wouldn't do that. God, I'd really like a cigarette.

'Excuse me,' I say, 'but are you a smoker?'

You look up from the engine. 'Not any more. I gave it up ten years ago.'

'Three years for me. I only miss it at times like this.'

You chuckle. 'You'll have to find another vice to replace it with.'

'Have you found one?'

You gaze down at the engine again. 'Not exactly.'

'Perhaps,' I say, 'we both need to find something else to give up.'

You straighten up and look at me. 'I think your timing's off.'

That takes me aback. 'Sorry,' I say.

'No, the engine timing. There's a belt inside that casing there. I need to take it off and have quick look. No worries. I'll just get my tools from the truck.'

Your car has broken down, and now we're having a little game. You're not wearing a wedding ring, but that doesn't always mean much. The inside of your car looks messy, but something tells me you haven't got kids, although that's just a hunch. I wonder why you're out here alone at this time of night, and I can't help feeling it suggests a touch of recklessness in your character. That could be interesting. There's something intense about you. You're pacing up and down, and maybe you lied about giving up smoking three years ago. Maybe you haven't given up at all. People often lie about that kind of thing, especially to themselves. I wonder what else you'll lie about.

'I know it's none of my business,' I say without looking up from the engine, 'but how do you come to be driving on a road like this in the middle of the night?'

You hesitate for a moment, then you say, 'I'm on my way to help a friend.'

'It's always good to help your friends.'

You say nothing, and I finish removing the casing around the timing belt. It looks like the belt needs adjusting. I'm just about to tell you to come and have a look, so I can show you what the problem is, when I hear your voice, surprisingly close behind me:

'Actually,' you say, 'it's a bereavement.'

'I'm sorry to hear that. Was it someone close?'

'Not to me, no. A good friend of mine just lost their partner, and I'm on my way to see them. But I wasn't close to the partner.'

Fair play, although there's something odd about the way you said that. Maybe you're not telling the whole story. Why would you? You don't know me. But there's an element of drama in the mix now, raising the stakes. Somebody has died, and they were close to a good friend of yours. Perhaps that's making you feel vulnerable. Although I'm not sensing vulnerability so much as restlessness.

I start adjusting the timing belt. 'So,' I say, 'did you leave in hurry?'

'What do you mean?'

I look up and nod towards the interior of the car, and give a friendly chuckle, and say, 'It looks like you just threw everything in the back!'

'Are you saying you think my car is a mess?'

I need to dial it back a little. 'No offence,' I say, 'and I only mention it because I have the same tendency. Why bother with a suitcase, when you've got all that space in the car, am I right?'

'Well, it's always like that. Nothing unusual about it for me.'

'Sorry, I didn't mean to imply anything.'

'That's all right. Will you be much longer?'

'Not long now,' I say, and get back to work.

My car has broken down, and I hope you won't take much longer to fix it. I need to be on my way. Mark is waiting for me, and he'll have finished what he was doing, and I need to get to him as soon as possible. He's only a few miles away, and I don't particularly want much more of your company. You're asking too many questions, and I'm answering too many of them. I don't like the way you've been glancing into the car, and I don't want you getting curious about what's under the blanket in the footwell between the front and back seats. I don't think you can really see it in the dark, but if you take it into your head to shine that lamp of yours in there, that could lead to problems.

Your car has broken down, but I'm adjusting the timing belt, no problem, so let's see where we're going with this.

'This belt will be OK for a while,' I say, 'but you'll need to get the whole thing replaced fairly soon.'

'All right,' you say. 'As long as it's going to work for now.'

'Absolutely. I wouldn't want you to break down again tonight, and certainly not on a road like this.'

'Thanks.'

'But I can understand if you're a bit nervous. Out here all by yourself.'

'I'm not by myself now, though, am I? You're here.'

'Very true.' I give a little laugh. 'But can you trust me?'

'What do you mean?'

'Well, for all you know, I might not be who I seem to be.'

'Who are you, then, if you're not who you seem to be?'

I laugh again, mostly to cover the fact that this wasn't the answer I expected. But that doesn't stop me moving on to the next stage, and saying, 'What if I'm some kind of maniac?'

'What kind of maniac would that be?'

I pause. You're standing directly behind me again, and I want you where I can see you. I adjust the lamp that's hanging off the open bonnet, and shuffle around. You take the hint, and move away. I smile. 'The kind of maniac,' I say, 'who uses their job as a vehicle breakdown engineer to target vulnerable people in lonely places.'

'Target them to do what?'

I look at you. Level gaze, giving nothing away. 'What do you think?'

'I really don't know,' you say, 'but I get the feeling you're trying to play some kind of game here, and I'm not interested.'

'What if it's not a game?'

'Then it's even more foolish.'

I nod slowly, and tighten the final nut. I pick up the timer belt casing from where it was resting against the bumper, and turn to you, holding the spanner in one hand and the casing in the other. A bit like a weapon and a shield, if you think about it. 'I'll tell you what I think is foolish,' I say. 'I think it's foolish to break down on a dark, lonely road in the middle of the night, and then to trust a complete stranger who arrives in a truck, and claims to have been summoned by the breakdown service, and not even ask to look at any identification. That strikes me as foolish.'

You laugh. It's not even a nervous laugh, that's the weird thing.

'If anything happens,' you say, 'you could be traced. There are records, like my phone call to the service, and they'll have a record of the call they put out for someone to take the job, even if you intercepted it and you're only pretending to work for a garage.'

'Really? Are you familiar with the case of that taxi driver? He drove a real London taxi cab, and was an actual cab driver, but he was still able to commit dozens of very serious assaults.'

'Yes, I am familiar with it. And you know why? Because he was caught.'

'Not for a long time,' I say, but my voice doesn't sound right.

You just stand there. You're not moving back, or looking scared, or anything like that. This isn't going the way I want, and although I don't blame myself it's probably best to drop it. You can't win them all. I start replacing the timer belt casing.

My car was broken down, and now it's fixed, and you've gone. I wonder why I feel so calm. I don't know exactly what game you thought you were playing, but I know you expected me to be scared. But I wasn't scared, and all the time it was happening I was watching us both, and finding it all rather amusing. Even when I was standing right behind you, with the crowbar held down close to my side, ready to move fast, I was observing myself. Perhaps I'm feeling this way because of what I've already done tonight. Should I worry about the fact that I've been seen out here, and there's a record of the car being here, just a few miles from where Mark has dug the hole? I don't think so. There's no way to connect me to Linda, because nobody knew about me and Mark. Even tonight, when I rang the doorbell at Mark and Linda's, wearing gloves, she had no idea who I was. When I said I was a friend of Mark's, I think she began to understand, but it was too late by then. And the hole will be very deep, Mark said. As for you, I don't think you'll be a problem. It's unlikely that Linda will ever be found, and even if it happens, I don't think you'll mention our encounter. You'd be forced to reveal too much about yourself. I don't know anything about the games you like to play, but I'm guessing you'd be ashamed, at the very least, if they came to light. And if they're more than just games, and I've had a lucky escape here tonight, there's all the more reason for you to keep quiet. On top of that, this car can't be connected to me, and soon it will be a lump of unrecognisable metal in a Liverpool scrapyard that asks no questions. I think everything will be all right. I haven't spoken to Mark tonight, as we don't want any phone records, but I'm thinking about him digging that deep hole, and working up a sweat, and I'm getting quite excited. Nearly there now.

The car seems to be working perfectly.

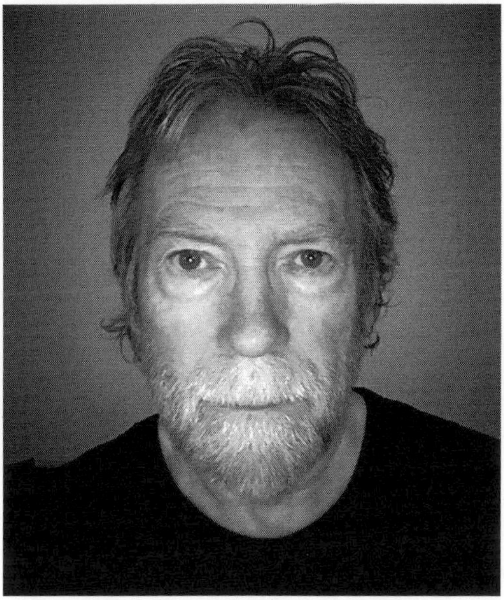

Paul Bassett Davies began his career in experimental multimedia before working in radio and television as a writer and producer. He has made several short films, and wrote music videos for Ken Russell and Kate Bush, and the screenplay for the feature animation film *The Magic Roundabout*. He is the author of four published novels and a collection of stories. He has also been the vocalist in a punk band, a DJ in a strip club and a cab driver.

Karen Jones

Breathing Patterns

Mammy's put into the council for a move to one of the houses in the electric scheme because, since the accident, Da can't even look at coal any more without his breathing going all funny and coal's all we have for heat here. Da's downstairs, drunk, singing 'Scarlet Ribbons'. He's never bought me scarlet ribbons – he's never bought me any ribbons – but at least he's not wailing 'Danny Boy' and at least Mammy's hidden the accordion. No one has seen the accordion for months. Maybe Mammy should have hidden the whisky in the same place.

In bed, listening to Da sing from the living room and Mammy clatter already clean pots in the kitchen, I hide my face under the covers and practise saying the bad words I've learned since I started high school. Just mouthing them, mind, in case my wee brother hears. I bite my bottom lip for the 'f' of 'fuck' and then open wide for the 'uh' sound and a noise slips out when I reach the 'ck'. I peek over to see if our Ian has heard, but he's saying his prayers, his hands pressed together at his chest, his eyes tight closed. Tam, his teddy bear, has its paws together as well, sitting there looking like his own personal priest. While Ian prays for us all to be blessed, I go back under the covers and try out 'bastard', but it's not as much fun as fuck.

Da's coughing now. It always happens after the singing because his lungs can't cope. He says he's like an accordion whose bellows have been attacked by moths, so instead of playing beautiful music, they just gasp and wheeze. It's because he has black lung, Mammy says, but how could she know that – how could she have seen his lungs in his chest? Mammy's like that – reckons she knows everything, or at least that's what Da says. Da says while he may have a black lung, she has a black heart but the bluest eyes he's ever seen, so he'll forgive her cruelty. She does have the bluest eyes and they tear up when he's nice to her like that, so it's just as well it doesn't happen very often.

Ian has finished his prayers and I know the questions are going to start.

'Our Claire, are you awake?'

I do the biggest, loudest snore. Ian laughs.

'Claire, why do you not say prayers any more? You'll go to the bad fire if you don't say your prayers every night and morning. That's what Father Rodgers says.'

I turn to face him. The space between our beds is so small, I can smell his toothpastey breath. 'I do so say my prayers. I just do it awful quiet, under the covers, so it's just me and God and no one else listening.'

'But who would listen? There's only me and Tam here, and we wouldn't eary-wig on you, would we, Tam?' He makes teddy Tam's head shake from side to side.

'Ach, I know, but I just like to be private sometimes. Now go to sleep – we've chores in the morning.'

Ian reaches his hand over to my bed and whispers, 'I don't want you to go to the bad fire, Claire – maybe you'd end up with black lungs like Da.'

I hold his hand, like I do every night to get him to sleep and promise there'll be no black lung and no bad fires. We'll be right as rain and he's not to bother his shirt worrying about anything Father Rodgers says.

Da's stopped coughing, so he starts up with the first verse of 'Dark Lochnagar'.

'Oh, Jesus,' I say.

Ian clamps his hand over his mouth for a second, then says, 'Our Claire! That's a sin, saying that!'

I laugh. 'Naw, naw, it's fine – it was just the start of a prayer and I was going to say, "Oh Jesus, please don't let him try to sing all the verses."'

Ian giggles, but I hear his breath slowing and know he's almost away.

I know everyone's breathing patterns. Da's broken accordion breaths, Mammy's exhausted huffs and puffs, Ian's quick, light breaths, then his sleepy wee snores. I wonder if any of them notice mine, hear how often I hold it and for how long. Mammy has noticed my chest is changing, growing and says we've to go to the shops in the morning to get me a training bra. I asked her what I'm in training for, but she told me I'm not as funny as I think I am. I wasn't trying to be funny; I just don't want a bra because I know everyone at school will make fun of me. If you've got a bra, they ping the straps and laugh at you 'cause you've got boobs. I'd rather just ignore the whole thing.

Ian's hand slips out of mine and I go back under the covers to try out the word 'tits'. I screw up my face because it doesn't sound nice. I feel where the bits of my chest are beginning to swell up and wish them away. But maybe wishing isn't enough. I make the sign of the cross and put my hands together and whisper, 'Dear God, can you fix Da's chest and make my chest go away. Ta. Oh, it's Claire, by the way – Claire McNeice.' I go back to saying fuck, trying out different voices, then remember I forgot to do a sign of the cross to finish my prayer, so I've been swearing at God. I feel the bad fire's flames nipping at my toes.

Mammy leaves a light on in the hall at night. She says it's for Ian, but I know it's for Da. He wakes up screaming if it's too dark, thinking he's back down there, everything collapsing around him. He was one of the few who made it out and he says he can't look anyone in the eye any more for the shame of being alive. A lot of stuff Da says doesn't make sense. The light shines on the statuettes we got as gifts for our First Communion. They frighten me, those porcelain children, on their knees, eyes raised to heaven, hands clasped at their chests, her communion dress and his suit perfectly pressed, her veil hanging straight, his sash bright red. I imagine they'll come to life one night, with those eyes that can't close, grow to full size and murder me and Ian for not being as good as them. They'll probably strangle us with our First Communion rosary beads, so everyone knows it was a message from God, which would be unfair on Ian, because he really does believe in all that bible stuff. I'm too old for that nonsense, though I'd never say that in front of Mammy. I hid the statuettes once – wrapped them up in the cloth they sit on and shoved them right to the back of the shelf in the cupboard. The next day they were back where they should be, and Mammy gave me a look as she dusted them. Hiding accordions and finding creepy statuettes – that's Mammy's magic powers.

In the morning, me and Ian start our chores. Because Da can't work any more, Ma is a cleaner in offices in the town, and on Saturdays she's worn out, so we've all to help. Ian's only wee, so he's just to set the table, but I'm nearly an adult, so I've to hang out the washing on the line, set the fire in the front room and then get the breakfast started.

Da comes back from the shop with his paper and the smell of Victory Vs on his breath. He ruffles Ian's hair and pinches my cheek, but then he sees there's specks of coal dust still under my fingernails and his face goes purple. I'm holding my breath again and his is rasping – even just the sight of the dust sets him off – so I run to the sink and get the nail brush and scrub and scrub and scrub until my fingers nearly bleed. I'm quick enough that the coughing doesn't start but he's got at least three Victory Vs in his mouth when Mammy comes into the room.

Mammy looks at Da, then looks at me and my hands, nods, and says, 'Right, well, a quiet morning, eh? C'mon, Claire – these eggs won't boil themselves.' It's enough, always enough, just her voice telling us everything is okay, and Da's colour is normal again – well, normal for him, which is red – and I can stop holding my breath and our Ian hasn't noticed a thing because he's too busy lining up the spoons and plates just so.

After breakfast, me and Mammy drop Ian off at Granny's and get the bus to Glasgow to buy my bra. She tells everyone who asks where we're going and I'm black affronted, but she doesn't notice or care. In the big shop where we go for our school uniforms, we go to the underwear department and she tells the woman why we we're there and the woman looks at me and says, 'Aw, going to be a big girl are ye, just like yer ma here?' I look at Mammy's chest and my eyes go wide and both Mammy and the shop woman laugh.

'Not for a while yet,' Mammy says, 'but best to get used to things now, eh?'

The woman brings out loads of tiny bras, all white. There's one that has wee flowers on it, so I hand it to Mammy and say, 'This one,' but she just pushes it to one side and says there's no need for anything fancy. She hands me what looks like a bandage with straps and shoves me over to the changing rooms.

I look at her like she's mad, which she must be if she thinks I'm going in behind that curtain. It reminds me of confession, where Father Rodgers tells you he knows your voice and he'll be telling your mammy all the bad things you've done.

Mammy taps her foot, a sure sign she's building a temper, and says, 'Hurry up! We'll miss the bus home if you dither about.'

In the changing room there's a full-length mirror. At home we only have the wee mirror above the bathroom sink for Da to see himself shaving and Mammy to do her lipstick, so I've never seen my whole self before. I'm skinny, which I already knew because everyone tells me, but I didn't know my legs were so long – or maybe this old skirt is just too short. I look like a baby giraffe in grey woollen tights. I don't know if I'm supposed to take off my top and vest or just try the bra over my own clothes, but I guess over, because who would be getting naked in a shop?

I put my arms through the straps and fasten the bra at the back, which isn't easy because the hooks are tiny. I shift it into place and look in the mirror. The bra puffs out where there's not enough to fill it. I know what's coming on Monday at school. I know the pointy bits will poke through my jumper and I know the boys will snap the straps and I know the girls will ask what colour it is and does it have flowers or frilly bits and I know, right there, right then, that I'd rather die. I take off the bra and run out of the changing room, out of the shop, all the way to the bus stop where I sit on the bench and wait for Mammy to arrive, to shout at me, to batter me, to drag me back to the shop.

I see her walking towards me, her back straight. She sits down on the bench, takes a big gulp of air, then holds my hand

and says, 'Maybe we can wait a few months yet.' I lean into her wool coat, breathing in the perfume she wears for special days – she must have thought this day was special – and whisper a thank you I'm not sure she hears. She puts her arm round me and says, 'We'll get the move soon and everything will be better. You'll see. He'll be better. He'll get another job. I'll be back at home for you and you can just be a wean again.' I don't know what me not getting a bra has to do with Da and work and moving house, but that's just how Mammy's mind works. She sniffs a tear away and takes a wee tub out of her bag and soothes creamy coldness onto my red raw hands where I scrubbed too hard this morning. And even though I can't see it, I know my mammy's heart is not black.

KAREN JONES is a flash and short story writer from Glasgow, Scotland. Her flashes have been nominated for Best of the Net, Best Micro Fiction and The Pushcart Prize, and her story 'Small Mercies' was included in *Best Small Fictions 2019* and BIFFY50 2019. She won first prize in the Cambridge Flash Fiction Prize, Flash 500, Reflex Fiction and Retreat West Monthly Micro in 2021. Her work has been published in numerous anthologies and magazines. Her novella-in-flash *When It's Not Called Making Love* is published by Ad Hoc Fiction. She's Special Features Editor at *New Flash Fiction Review*.

Peter Burns

The Ghost of Your Words

'Promise me you'll stick in at school, get a good job and get the hell out of here,' Jacko says, early morning in the tenement close.

You shiver, cold from the concrete step corkscrewing up through your buttocks and into your back. Jacko puts an arm around you, pulls you in tight, and you say, 'I promise.'

'That's my man. Now get your arse out there. The boys are waiting.'

Tenements spaced in oval arrangement. The square sits dead centre and a road circles it. Like an amphitheatre, you thought, that day you and Tommo were fighting and all around you kids stood cheering and up above you, faces filled the windows. Big drops of blood as you ran towards your tenement. Jacko coming through the door, telling you to pinch your nose. The look of disappointment on your father's face, knuckles whitening around his whisky glass. Tommo's punch the first of the day, the one to set the pace.

'Keep your fists up like this,' Jacko says. 'Elbows in tight at your chest. Jab first with your left and then hook hard with your right.'

The back garden green like a boxing ring, poles in each corner, washing lines above our heads.

The ball bounces high towards you, before you've even set foot onto the cracked concrete slabs.

'In with the noggin,' Davie says.

You leap and twist but the ball sails overhead.

Tommo laughs. 'That was a shite effort.'

The ball comes to rest against the wheel of Mr McLean's car. Look left and right like Ma still tells you, even though you've just hit your teens.

'Too focused on the bloody ball, that's why I need to keep telling you. Don't know how many times I've seen you, or one of your daft pals, almost flattened by some maniac wanting home pronto for his dinner.'

Ma grunts as she turns the handle. Wet jeans squish through the wringer and you imagine those same jeans under wheels, only with your legs in them.

You pick up the ball and see a half-brick lying under Mr McLean's car.

'Maybe better just passin' the ball back to us,' Tommo says, behind you. 'Then take yerself off for a game of ropes with the lassies.'

Even Davie's laughing, and he's your best pal. The half-brick is easy to reach; you don't have to get down on your knees.

'Never let anyone put you on your knees,' Da says. 'Not even me.'

Back against the wall, trying to stay upright. But still, your legs begin to buckle.

'Do you hear me?' Da says.

You enclose the pain his fist has left with your arms, like you're trying to keep your stomach from slipping out – jelly through fingers. You slide to the floor.

'You don't want to end up like me,' Jacko says, in the cold, concrete morning on the tenement close stairs.

You pick up the half-brick and turn.

'Only nineteen and he's spent nine months in prison already,' Da says. 'I don't want you anywhere near that Jacko one.'

'He's just a big, daft boy really,' Ma says. 'Christ, it was only a couple of years ago he was playing cops and robbers with James and his pals.'

'Aye, that was like an apprenticeship for the daft bastard. Well, he's time served now.'

Tearing through the back greens, guns in hand. You and Jacko the robbers; Tommo and Davie hot on your heels. White flashes of wet linen whipping in the wind. Women shouting from kitchen windows to watch what the hell you're doing. Jacko vaults Da's garden fence. You shoot a glance over your shoulder, up at your own windows.

'Get in here, before they clock you,' Jacko says.

Saturday. Football on the television; whisky in his hand. You join Jacko to lie between the rows of Da's potatoes.

You wake with a jolt – sound of a spade slicing through frozen soil. You sit up and part your bedroom curtains. Silhouette in Da's garden, down on its knees. Something planted, rises and turns. You know him by his walk.

'Promise you'll never become like me. Promise me you'll stick in at school and get a good job and get the hell out of here.'

You kick the ball to Davie and walk towards Tommo, the half-brick in your hand.

'Think you can hack it with the big boys, do you?' Tommo says.

You toss the half-brick into the air and catch it.

They're running through the tenement doorway, guns held high. Hit the wall; slide their backs up it; take the stairs slowly with guns pointed upwards.

You arc the half-brick downwards.

'Promise me.'

The half-brick slams onto a concrete slab across from another one like it.

'Here's the goals,' you say, as Tommo smiles. 'So take your best shot.'

You get your fingertips to the ball and nudge it past the half-brick. It bounces and rolls off the square. You punch the air, give Tommo the finger and move for the road. Screech of a motor at high speed, faces suddenly at windows, and you're in the amphitheatre again with the brutal fear of it all bearing down upon you.

The first motor breaks before you, the second swerves and mounts the pavement. Car doors thrown wide and men spill out from all sides. With heads low and guns held high, they sprint towards your tenement. You follow without thinking.

Inside, their backs hit the wall, sliding up it as they take the stairs, slowly. One of them turns, sees you and pokes a finger towards the tenement doorway.

A spectator like the others, you stand on the square and wait. They bring Jacko out stripped to the waist, hands cuffed at his back, push his head down into the first car. It leaves and the other stays.

From your bedroom window you watch the plainclothes policemen dig up Jacko's garden. You know they won't find anything.

Later, that night, when they have given up their search, you slip out and head down into the back gardens, Da's spade in your hand. Digging up his potatoes, you know, will lead to more hurt than any pain you've ever felt. The spade strikes something and you force it up from the ground. A black bin bag. Opening it, you pull out more money than you will ever see again. Yet something else lies there, metallic and heavy and cold and so real to the touch it threatens to punch a hole straight through the world, straight through your life.

Torchlight from behind and your shadow splashes over the ground.

'Gently place it to your right and lie face down.'

Plainclothes policemen creeping through the back greens, guns in hand.

You stand and turn, still holding it, like it's a part of you now. Like it's the part of you you've been missing all of your short life.

Something rips through your chest, exits your back, takes your breath with it, and you're thrown backwards onto the compost heap in the corner, the last of you filtering down through used teabags and rotting fruit to warm and soften the cold, hard soil.

'Maybe I could become your partner,' you say to Jacko on the tenement close step, that cold, cracked, concrete morning.

'You don't want to end up like me,' Jacko says, 'Christ, I'm nineteen and already been banged up.'

'But people give you respect. Nobody messes with you.'

'Yeah, but that kinda respect doesn't cut it inside, James. And it's no bloody use to anybody when they're dead. Is it? No, you need to promise me. Promise me you'll stick in at school, get a good job and get the hell out of here. Promise me.'

'I promise,' you say, watching the vapour rising from your mouth like the ghost of your words.

Peter Burns holds a master's degree in creative writing, with distinction, and a BA (Hons) in literature, both from the Open University. He won first place in the Flash 500 competition in November 2020, after several years of being shortlisted and longlisted. He has been shortlisted in the Flash 500 short story competition and longlisted in the TSS Cambridge Prize for Flash Fiction as well as having previously been longlisted in the Bath Short Story Award. He has stories published in *FlashBack Fiction* and *FlashFlood* journal for National Flash Fiction Day.

Maria Clark

Georgie Three

Me mam picked the name.

She liked the kings, you see. Pa says she should be happy that there's a woman on the throne, but Mam just grumbles, saying that woman or not, Queen Vic lives a completely different life to us. I remind her that even the Queen has a big family like ours, but Mam just snorts.

Like she looks after her own children, Georgie.

I'm Georgie, Georgie Three.

Gracie Blackwell across the yard bet me thruppence that I wouldn't make it this far, but I'll be six-and-a-half this autumn. I'm smaller than her, and much smaller than my brothers and sisters, but Pa says that I have this look in my eyes, this look of determination, that means I'm not going anywhere just yet.

Georgie One was the original. He was Mam's firstborn, a regular George, nice and tall. Me mam says that he must have been eavesdropping from her tummy, 'cause he came out the perfect child, with the perfect manners and brains.

He worked at White Cross Mill. Pa wanted him to help in the port, but even he was struggling to get work, and Mam didn't like the idea of another man coming home, stinking of the silt and rusted iron of the old ships. Cotton-spinning, she told Georgie One, was a growing industry and he would find himself in very high demand, once he learnt the right skills.

Gladys works there now. I sometimes go to meet her, standing a bit out the way, hidden in the shadows. The men that come out are weary and frustrated, coughing their lungs out. You can smell the heat and the raw, burnt materials even when the doors are closed, and the chimneys pump steam into the air. If I'm early, I like watching it as it slips into the sky, escaping to the stars. It's the only thing that ever fully leaves that place.

Gladys tries not to cough at home, but it's only a matter of time. That's what happened with Georgie One. The cough grew and grew, and at night, Mam could hear him spluttering in his pillow. Edward and Victor said nowt about it but every day his face got paler, like the off-white of my nightdress.

He never complained, Mam tells me. He was always worried about the others – there were six of them, at that point – and even after his hearing went, from the noise of the machines, he learnt to lipread his brothers and sisters.

I never met him. He died when I was born. I was supposed to be called Elsie originally, but in her grief, mam changed her mind. So I'm Georgie, Georgie Three.

Gracie Blackwell's mam always laughs when I tell her.

You're supposed to use the name again when they're still alive, she says, hanging her washing across the courtyard. She has a right funny way of boiling it. Mam hates the smell.

How else can the new Georgie learn from the old?

I don't mind having the same name. Mam tells me so many stories about Georgie One that sometimes I think he's standing next to my bed, or watching me playing in the yard.

But it's not fun having a birthday when it's also a Death Day.

It's my birthday tomorrow. I was born at two o'clock in the morning, and Georgie One died at three. I was Elsie for an hour, but it wasn't long enough to stick.

I'm Georgie Three, now.

Mam always tries hard with birthdays. It's difficult when she's got to feed and clothe and bathe all nine of us – Baby doesn't seem to get any older, either – but she'll always save a bit, for a special tea.

When I wake up, I can already smell the broth boiling. It's still dark out, and the cold rattles on the window sill. Ivy is asleep next to me and she flops over, her breath sour against my cheek.

Georgie Two prods my shoulder.

You awake, pet?

I nod.

She slips out of bed, leaving a sliver of warmth. I can see her bare feet against the floorboards, toes wiggling. When she lights a candle, her face is thin, with deep ink-blotches beneath her eyes.

You tell Ma I'll be back late, she says. I've got a surprise for you.

If Georgie One was perfect, Georgie Two is almost there. She's sharp-tempered and feisty, and the big black boots she wears to the market could knock anyone down with one blow. But she's very sweet, really, and always tries to help our mam when she's busy.

I wonder what the surprise could be. New boots? I need a coat, and new boots, but I can't have both at once. With nine of us, that would be a miracle.

Mam's waiting downstairs.

Happy birthday, love, she says, kissing me. Her lips are dry and hard, but at least they're warm.

Pa's gone to the port, but he'll be back for tea. I'll promise yer that.

Her eyes soften.

Six, hey? And to think that's six years of our Georgie passing.

She picks up Baby, pressing him against her breast. She's trying not to cry, but I know exactly what to do.

And may he be at rest with the Lord in heaven, I say.

Mam turns back around, pasting a smile on her face, like the ads stuck in the paper.

Alreet, love – you go off now, she says.

Georgie Two's already gone, I say, sniffing the broth. It's for a surprise.

There's a twinkle of excitement in me, but I push it down.

Mam laughs.

Surprise? In this house? A likely story.

The courtyard stinks, even at this hour. We're close to the river, for Pa's work, and the seagulls are wheeling and turning overhead, the wind buffeting them across the town.

I'm supposed to be at school, but who wants to go on their birthday?

It's market day. The stalls are crammed together, and the crowds start to choke the rows. I look for Georgie Two, but she's not here. The air is thick with the smoke from the chestnut stand, and I try not to inhale. It's hours until tea.

I hope Mam makes some oatcakes. She does them just the way I like, perfectly browned in the pan, with a tiny knob of butter on top. If we're lucky.

I go to the port. There's only one ship there, leaning on its side, dozing against the bank. There's a great clamour of workers surrounding it, fighting for the chance to get some work. Pa's probably there too, but he'll get on. He's got just the knack of elbowing people. He says it comes from his days of street-fighting as an urchin.

The river's a muddy colour today. The water barely moves, and the sun only skims the surface. I think of the map in the schoolhouse with all the rivers and mountains marked on it. Do they all slop against the shore, smelling of dirt and sewage and all that?

Someone runs past me. The doctor's boy.

Summat the matter? I say.

He slows. He's a James, a James Two, but his family call him Jem. There's nowt but George for a boy.

It's a good thing me and Georgie Two were girls, then.

Jem's walking now, but he doesn't stop.

There's another case of cholera, he says. You watch out, Georgie.

I shiver.

Gracie Blackwell's brother died of cholera. I remember peeping in their window, seeing him lying down. Mam was terrified and wouldn't let me go inside, but you could hear his moans through the walls.

I go past the infirmary on the way home. It's much better to go round the back than the front, 'cause you really see what's happening. If me mam knew, she would kill me on the spot.

There's a big black cart outside, with two horses, tapping their hooves nervously. I stand on my tiptoes to look in the back and then jump back quickly, sick rising in my tummy.

A pile of white-covered bodies stares up at me.

Hey! What do you think you're doing?

Hands grab my waist and fling me away from the cart. I land on my knees on the cobbles, my dress tearing down the side.

The man glares at me.

Don't you know better than to disturb the dead?

The dead. They look like Georgie Two, when she's sleeping: lying flat on her back, gazing up at the ceiling as if she can see God through her eyelids.

I try not to think about the cause of their deaths. It could be anything. Disease is so common in these parts that Pa likes to call it his tenth child. Skulking in the corner, stealing his last pennies.

Besides, the man continues, do you want to spread it further?

It's definitely cholera.

I decide not to tell me mam.

Gladys and Victor are waiting for me. They've made newspaper decorations for the table, and Mam's laid her best tea set. She's put her best dress on, too, and tied her apron over it, so it doesn't get covered in flour. Her fingers look like they've been speckled with snow.

Pa comes in, just as the oatcakes are ready.

Where's Georgie Two? Mam says, when everyone's at the table.

The door bangs open, and Georgie Two bursts in, holding a steaming pot wrapped in her petticoats.

What ye got there, love? Pa says.

Georgie Two puts it in the centre of the table and beams at me. She's sweating, and her hair sticks to her face like strands of seaweed.

It's for Georgie Three, she says.

Mam opens the lid and we all sigh. A steaming pot of cockles, perfectly cooked and ready to eat.

From the market? Mam says.

Georgie Two shakes her head, breathing quickly.

I got them from the river meself, she says. And then Mrs Blackwell let me cook at hers.

I give her a big kiss, beaming. She knows how much I love cockles.

Did you hear about the cholera, Ma? Georgie Two says, shifting on her seat.

Me mam stiffens, and takes a deep breath.

Let's not spoil Georgie's day, shall we?

When I wake up in the morning, Georgie Two is sitting on the edge of the bed, holding her stomach. She's shivering, but when I touch her hand, she's hotter than a factory chimney.

Is summat wrong? I say.

She tries to smile.

I'm sure it's nothing.

Then, before I've even pulled off the blanket, she runs out the room and is sick outside.

Ivy rolls over and looks at me. She's been awake the entire time.

Do you think…?

Don't, I say, rubbing the blanket between my fingers. Don't even say it.

It only takes two days.

Two days and two nights of burning skin, parched lips and a bucket by the bed. I sit by her side, pressing a damp cloth against her forehead, and praying. Just praying.

We bury her in the morning. There's no time to make mourning dresses, or to even beg a black ribbon from the haberdashers. Ma wears her best dress. It still smells of cockles.

When they've lowered her into the ground, me mam turns to me. Her cheeks are wet, and she grabs my hand, squeezing it like she's afraid I'll go too.

Georgina, she says. You've got to make them proud, alreet? Both of them.

I look up at the sky. They're up there, watching over me, and the others. I know it.

I never minded being number three. It was nice to have two older siblings, ready to help me and show me the way.

But now it's different.

I'm the only Georgie now.

MARIA CLARK is a writer and lover of languages, travel, photography and history. As a third-year English literature and creative writing student at Lancaster University, her work has been published by *Bandit Fiction* and *CP Quarterly*, and other achievements include winning the First Story National Writing Competition (2016), and being shortlisted for the Iggy&Litro Young Writers' Prize (2017) and the Sunderland Short Story Award (2018). She is currently seeking representation for her debut novel. As well as writing, Maria loves travelling, spending time with family and exploring new cultures. She is particularly excited to move to the Netherlands this summer to undertake a work-based placement.

R. J. Lingard

Dead End

'Stop.' The Red Man rubs his forehead once more and repeats his question.

'I asked you where you were between the hours of ten and two last night? I'm not waiting any more. Tell me what happened.'

Amber doesn't look up.

She clasps her hands together and fidgets in her seat. The Red Man thumps the table then jabs a finger at her. 'Answer the question.'

'I don't know, we were out late, we went to a few bars, my head's fuzzy, I can't remember most of it.'

'Not good enough.' He leans over the cheap veneer table and grits his red teeth. 'That dim bulb of yours better start thinking up a story, quick, otherwise it's you that's going down for this.'

Amber still doesn't look up.

She looks at the floor, at the dull, grey carpet and the plastic flap that covers the plug sockets beneath the floor. Only, it doesn't cover the plug sockets. Instead, the flap is up, resting its weight on a brown power cable that snakes up the wall and into the back of the tape recorder. She hopes she never has to hear her voice replayed through that thing in traffic court.

The Red Man slaps the table once more before turning his back. He takes a red pen from his red pocket and jabs it between two horizontal blinds. There's a mist on the window, condensation so thick a draught whistles through his teeth. They're still clenched. Still angry. Still red.

'Perhaps we might look at this from another angle?' The Green Man places down a beige coffee and dips his head so Amber can see his smile. His luscious green smile. 'Look, Amber, nobody is accusing you of anything.'

'I am,' says The Red Man.

'All we have are the facts, and the facts tell us one thing and your story tells us another.' The Green Man opens his notebook and runs his finger down a list of bullet points. All written in green ink. 'The three of you were at work until ten o'clock last night.'

Amber relaxes her shoulders a little and places her palms on the table.

'That's correct,' she says. 'We're only part-time signals. On at six a.m., off at ten p.m.'

The Red Man gives a huff.

The Green Man continues. 'Right. Then you went out, and we have witnesses who say they saw you drinking at The Weak Bridge, The Staggered Junction and The Hidden Dip. That's all fine. After that, I'm in the dark as to which route you took. You say you then went on to a pop-up bar by the name of Loose Chippings before finishing up at a club called Urban Clearway.' He takes a sip of his coffee as he finishes recapping the night. 'That's quite the night out, when you have work in the morning.' He turns to his partner, 'don't you think?'

The Red Man shakes his head. 'Quite the night. Bloody part-timers.'

Amber turns her palms up and sees that her sweat has left a sticky residue on the table. 'It's the truth,' she says. 'We had tickets for the gig at the Urban Clearway, just ask Red Light.'

'Interesting.' The Green Man clicks his pen. 'Which band did you see?'

'Joy Diversion. They are, I mean, they were, Green Light's favourite.'

She sniffles.

'So, after this event you and Red Light got into a cab around midnight and left Green Light out on her own. You went home and it was lights out until we arrived to pick you up. Is that correct?'

Amber flickers. 'It was round about then, yes. Green Light wanted to stay out after the gig, Red Light wanted to call it a night. I didn't know what to do, but, in the end, I decided it was probably best to turn in for the night.'

The Green Man taps his fingers on the table. 'Was there anyone else with you?'

'No.'

Amber's response is a little quick for his liking. He lays down his notepad and sits forward. He takes a photograph out from an evidence bag and slides it across to her.

'For the purposes of the tape I am showing the suspect evidence item P, a photograph captured by CCTV from the Quayside taxi rank.' He taps the picture. 'Amber, could you describe what you see in this image?'

Amber's fingertips slide onto the picture, she pulls it closer. The image is grey, pixelated, and unclear. She looks down at herself and then the memory flashes back.

'It shows Red Light, Green Light and me getting into a cab.'

'That's correct, Amber.' The Green Man nods. 'Now, as you can see, the image lacks colour, so, I'm hoping you can help illuminate The Red Man and myself as to who this is?'

The Green Man's green pen taps on the upper right corner of the image. Amber brightens and peers in. It's difficult to make out. Then she spots it. A fourth bulb on the other side of the taxi. It's hard to detect but it's there. Watching them.

'I… I don't know.' She rubs her eyes.

The Green Man stares at her.

'I don't, I swear.' Amber's bulb is flickering, her eyes fizz with tears. 'It's the truth, you've got to believe me. I didn't do anything. Haven't you spoken to Red Light? She'll say the same thing.'

'We tried that. Now we're asking you.' The Red Man doesn't so much as say the words as spit them out and volley them across the room like pieces of used chewing gum.

'He's not wrong,' says The Green Man. 'We spoke to Red Light. Well, he did, and we found that Red Light and The Red Man just make things, well, redder.'

Confusion glows across Amber's face.

'Think carefully, you're at a crossroads now,' says The Green Man.

She stays silent.

The Green Man looks back at his notes whilst The Red Man spots a glimmer of purple in the distance. For most, it's the dawn of a new day, for him it's a bruise coming to the surface. He clenches his fists.

'That's it. I'm done waiting, Green Man.' He turns to Amber. 'I've had enough of your U-Turns. I want to know who this bulb is right now.' He pounces on the table. Red arms planted like two great oaks, his red tie a pendulum between them. He yanks another image from the file and holds it in front of her. 'Look at her.'

'No. Stop, please.'

'How does she end up like this?'

'I don't know, I don't know.' Amber arches her back, the tears are causing jolts across her body. She howls as The Red Man shoves the picture into her face.

'How does she end up like this? Face down on the side of the highway, broken into a thousand pieces.'

Amber is flashing now, humming, and buzzing. Racing with emotion. All she can see is The Red Man's face, all she can smell is his breath – it reeks of tobacco and last night's lager. She twists to the side and looks to The Green Man for help. He's still inspecting his notes when he catches her gaze. Green teeth flash as he gives her a sympathetic smile.

The Red Man snarls. 'Don't look at him. He's not going to help you.'

Amber backs her chair up further. The wall is on her before she knows it and, even though it's solid, it feels like it's attacking her. She's trapped in a pincer movement between bad breath and bad plastering.

The Red Man is becoming scarlet, about to ignite. 'Tell me. Now. Who is it? Who was with you?'

She's suffocating. There's no escape, the flickering intensifies. She feels herself surging, about to pop, when the words blurt from her mouth. 'Left Turn Filter.'

A bomb goes off in the room.

The words knock The Red Man back so hard his legs give way, he collapses into his chair. The Green Man dives into the case file, thumbing back and forth through the pages, trying to find the answer to the question he knows he's forgotten to ask.

'My god.' He pulls out a piece of paper and slides it across to his colleague.

It's a report. A standard road works report. One he's looked at ninety-nine times. Only this is that one-percenter; this is the one time when he didn't read the details. The devil is hiding there, winking back at him.

'How did we miss this?' says The Red Man.

'It was installed a week ago,' Amber says as she breaks down in tears. 'There was too much traffic building up on the slip road. It backed up onto the motorway. We had to do something to ease congestion. So, we brought in an extra pair of hands.'

'Well, I'll be…' The Green Man loses his train of thought.

The Red Man shakes his head. 'It's obvious. How could we be so stupid?'

Amber weeps. 'Please, you must protect me, if she finds out it was me that told you…' She looks at the picture of Green Light. The chalk line around her body.

The glass, so much glass.

The Red Man buries his head in his hands. The Green Man gets to his feet. Amber feels a change in the room, it's depressurising, like an airplane fuselage that's just had a bullet rip through one of its windows.

A screech rips across the room as The Green Man pulls out the top drawer of a rusty filing cabinet. He takes out a brown folder so thick the filing cabinet breathes a sigh of relief as it's removed. It lands on the desk with a thud.

'What is that?' asks Amber.

The Red Man refuses to look at her. He folds his red arms like a level crossing sign and looks up at the ceiling. A cheap fan spins above him.

'This is everything we have on Left Turn Filter. We've been hunting her for years.' The Green Man opens the folder, and a tsunami of papers flood the desk. Dozens of crime scene photos, grainy and glossy, full of shattered signs and broken bulbs. On top of that are witness statements, evidence logs and a police artist's sketch of Left Turn Filter.

'That's her.' Amber pushes the drawing away. 'She said she'd shatter me if I said anything.'

'What a mess.' The Red Man pinches his red nose.

The Green Man says, 'She's managed to evade us at every turn, she's broken the highway code more times than a getaway driver.' He flips the file to the back and adds Amber's statement to it.' And now it seems she's done it again.' The Green Man lets out a sigh, his head hangs over the mess of papers. 'I think our investigation just hit another roadblock.'

There's silence until Amber says, 'Why does she do it?'

'Power.' The Red Man pushes his chair back and walks over to the window.

The Green Man elaborates. 'She's been doing this for years. Up and down the highways. Always one junction ahead of us. We believe it's Green Light envy. A condition where the Green Light has the power to allow all traffic to move, whereas the Left Turn Filter, although green, only has the power to allow one lane to move. She always works alone and is often trialled, temporary or, in some cases, simply ignored.'

'Oh my god,' Amber shakes her head and wipes her tears. 'She's a monster.'

'Indeed. But don't worry.' The Green Man collects the papers up and puts the file back. 'We'll get you the protection you need.'

Amber's bulb begins to brighten. 'So, what does that mean for me?' She looks at the two men.

The Red Man, hands on hips, stares at her without emotion.

The Green Man walks to the door. He opens it, smiles, and says, 'You're free to go.'

R. J. LINGARD grew up in Sheffield, England. After studying film at university, he spent most of his twenties living and working abroad in Canada, Thailand and Hong Kong. Upon returning to the UK, he established a career in digital marketing and began building a self-publishing business in his spare time. After six years of hard work, he left his day job to concentrate on his side business and pen his debut novel. Outside of writing, he spends his time reading, listening to heavy metal and watching American football. He currently lives in Stockport with his wife and two children.

Rupert Tebb

The Mountain Range Behind the Clothes Rack

B&Q is surprisingly busy for Christmas Eve. Couples in matching elf-hats load trolleys with cut-price decorations. Plastic angels ascend from towers of power tools. A huge snowman, made of tent material, slowly inflates and deflates with the wheezing sound of an impossibly old, impossibly slow ventilator, like a patient on life support.

Dad is waiting for me in front of the animatronic reindeer. The soft-toy heads bob and sway as they sing Christmas Classics. Their mouths open and close, almost but not quite in time with the music, like a bad lip-syncing act. Dad bobs and sways too, mouthing the verse but surer of the chorus. He waves as I get closer.

'Great aren't they,' he says.

We stand side by side, watching them perform. When the music finishes the heads freeze for a moment and their jaws hang slack. The next track starts up.

'Oh my god, are they singing "Baby, it's Cold Outside"?' I say.

'I think so.'

'Wow. Creepy.'

'What do you mean?'

I hold my finger to my lips and we both listen to the lyrics.

'She clearly wants to go,' I say, 'and he won't let her.'

'What?'

'It's a bit date-rapey … not letting her go home.'

'Date-rapey reindeer?'

'And then there's the line about the spiked drink.'

He looks at me blankly. I open my mouth to say something and then think better of it. 'Doesn't matter.'

We wander around, picking up the things we need. My dad is in his element. He engages in detailed discussions with the staff about the best approach for each job, the tools he might need and the pros and cons of every product: a conversation of nouns and imperatives I have to force myself to follow.

After my shift, I head home. Only the odd lifts are working, so I go up to the thirteenth floor then take the stairs back down to the twelfth. Dad meets me at the door and takes me on a tour of his handiwork; in the kitchen he opens and closes the window and I listen, appreciatively, to the rumble of the trains below stop and start; in the bathroom he shows me the mould-free sealant, white against the veal-coloured sink and bath; then he pauses dramatically outside the living room door before opening it with a flourish.

Inside, a tacky, light-up, 100% plastic, environmental-disaster, late-stage-capitalism, lawn-ornament reindeer illuminates the room with flashing LEDs. I hang onto my smile, but the reindeer is the least of my worries. The room is full of Christmas trees. Not just one or two, but thirty or forty. Large trees stand against the wall, the tops straining at the ceiling. Medium trees crowd the sofa and frame the window. Small trees circle the coffee table.

An entire forest in a council flat.

'On sale,' he says, grinning. 'Only a pound each, be rude to leave them in the shop.'

'Dad,' I say.

'Not much use for them,' he says, 'like Easter eggs after Easter.'

I bite my tongue.

For dinner we eat deep-pan, meat-feast on the sofa, watch Christmas specials, and try to ignore the whole woodland scenario. After a couple of cans, the sourness at the back of my throat recedes and I allow myself to thaw a little.

When I go to fetch his sleeping bag, I flick the overhead lights on. The whole scene is reflected in the window, obliterating the world outside. The duplicated room floats in the air beyond the glass, a forest conjured into being twelve storeys above the railway tracks. Our shadow selves hang there too, levitating in the dark with no safety net to catch them.

I wonder if we will hug each other.

The next morning, I make tea for my dad and take it in. There's an odd, overcast light in the room and I can feel cold emanating from the walls, like I'm standing in the open doorway of a display freezer. I squeeze through the trees to fiddle with the thermostat. Dad sits cross-legged, the sleeping bag wrapped around him like a shawl, warming his hands on the mug. I open a box of premium mince pies, recommended in *The Metro*, and we eat them for breakfast.

'It's really pine-y smelling,' he says. '*Really* pine-y.'

'Yeah,' I say, 'like someone pepper-sprayed you with air-freshener.'

He laughs and rubs his balding calves.

'Sounds weird in here too,' I say. 'Kinda muffled.'

I think I see snowflakes falling lazily from the ceiling. I squint up but it looks normal: stained Artex swirls over bad plasterwork. I look at my dad to see if he's noticed, but he seems oblivious.

I give him a pair of Niwaki secateurs that he seems genuinely pleased with, although the whole Japanese aspect probably escapes him. He gives me shapeless, straight-boy pants that make me wonder how anyone is ever conceived. We watch a bit of *Wallace and Gromit* and then I order Christmas dinner from the local Indian, a tradition left over from the time when Mum was too ill to cook.

It's getting much harder to ignore the snow now, which is starting to settle across everything and drift around the legs of the coffee table. The walls seem less solid, and a gentle breeze is twitching the aluminium food containers. Between the flashing reindeer and the TV, a small path has opened up into a forest beyond.

'Can you see that?' I say and point.

'Lovely,' he says, seemingly unfazed by the transformation.

He searches out his slippers, picks them up with his toes, drops them neatly side by side and pushes his feet in.

'Fancy a Christmas Day stroll?' he says.

'No,' I say. 'Don't be daft.'

'You sure?'

'Positive.'

'Suit yourself.'

He stands up and starts down the path.

'Your slippers will get soaked,' I shout after him, but he doesn't hear, and I watch him disappear from sight.

When he comes back down the path later that afternoon, it's dusk. He steps carefully past the radiator and stands in front of the TV dressed in a crazy full-length fur coat and fur boots.

'What are you wearing?' I ask.

'Great, isn't it?' He turns to show me the back. 'Reindeer, I think. Super warm.'

'Poor Rudolph.'

'I think you'll find it's Prancer.'

I raise my eyebrows and smile but try not to encourage him too much.

'How did you get it?'

'Traded it with some of the old boys over the ridge,' he says and points to the mountain range behind the clothes rack. 'I do repairs for them.'

He pushes back the hood and I see that he looks much, much older than he was this morning.

'Jesus,' I say. 'Are you ok?'

'Yes,' he says. 'Best move I ever made. You should come visit. There's someone I'd like you to meet.'

'You only left a couple of hours ago.'

'Funny. Stick the kettle on, I'm parched.'

By the time I get back, he's gone. I stand in the doorway, mist rising from the cup of tea in my hand. The room is just a room, quiet and still; the vast, unknowable landscape has vanished. A dull pain builds at the back of my throat. I hold myself motionless, scared to let go of this moment, unwilling to restart time.

The trees have begun to brown and wither.

Soon they will be dead, and I will have to remove them one by one. Each day, I will pick the sickliest. I will carry it along the corridor and take it down in the lift. I will abandon it at the end of the service road, by the bins, where it will wait for the council to collect it. I will spend hours hoovering the needles from the carpet, picking up the bulk of them using the normal attachment, then switching to the smaller, angled nozzle to get the stubborn ones that have lodged themselves between the carpet and the wall. I will resign myself to a lifetime as a human pincushion. I will leave the plastic reindeer till last, manically flashing its message between worlds, before, finally, I pack it away under my bed.

Rupert Tebb pilfers bits from queer theory and speculative fiction to write tall tales about twenty-first-century realities. He splits his time between London and Sanday, a remote Orcadian island with a history of radicalism. Earlier this year he won the DISQUIET Prize for literature. His work is published in *Granta* and *Litro*.

Emily Devane

On the Beauty of Sad Endings

Norman turns up to Alice's mask party dressed as the Invisible Man. I find him by an open window, plotting his escape. He's made quite the effort.

'It's the ultimate mask,' he says.

'Very clever,' I reply. 'But the cravat?'

'I was going for the Claude Rains look.' Norman sips his beer through a candy-striped straw. He's having difficulty on account of the tight bandaging around his mouth. 'It was his voice that swung it for him. For Rains, I mean. Everything was set for Boris Karloff to play the part – you know the guy, the one who played Frankenstein?' He takes another sip of his beer.

'I wasn't sure you'd come. Alice didn't think you'd make it, and neither did I ... Norm, do you want me to fix those bandages? You can't even talk properly!' I reach out to touch his face but he waves away my hand and I retreat, arms shimmering limply at my sides. The light is soft.

'Lou, you look … incredible,' he says. 'That stuff on your eyes. It's…'

'Like I've been dead two thousand years?' My Cleopatra mask hangs down my back. I can see myself in the curved glass of his shades – the ones he bought in a hurry at Luton Airport. I resemble a trapped fly.

Norman laughs, as much as is possible with a face covered in bandages. 'I was going to say 'authentic'. It's a coincidence, you coming like this. Claude Rains played Caesar to Vivien Leigh's Cleopatra.'

I nod, though it's disconcerting not being able to see his eyes beneath the sunglasses.

He leans forward. 'Imagine we're in a dark room and I'm a floating voice,' he says.

'We already are in a dark room,' I say. 'No need to imagine.'

Norman leans even closer. Beer is heavy on his breath.

'Norm…' The smell of beer is making me queasy. I cast around and spot Bev passing by with a tray of cocktail sausages on sticks. 'Hey, Bev, have you two met?'

'I'm Norman,' says Norman.

Bev's hair has been back-combed at the crown. She resembles George Michael in the 'Careless Whisper' video. 'If you say so,' she says, peering at Norman's bandaged face, 'but really, you could be anyone. What a great way to gatecrash a party!'

'He was invited,' I say, 'by Alice.'

'I was,' says Norm, and I can tell from the slump of his shoulders he's a little wounded by the suggestion he shouldn't be here.

'I'm kidding,' says Bev. 'Will a sausage ruin your face?'

'Did you know,' I say, 'George Michael wore sunglasses to avoid having to speak to people, like Norm here?'

Norman laughs. Turns out Bev has come as Lady Di. I hadn't spotted the silk blouse with the bow at the neck and the cardboard Lady Di face resting on top of her head. I mouth the word 'sorry', make an excuse about needing air and before they have even clocked my departure, I'm through the patio door. I grab a handful of crisps on my way and cram them in my mouth when no one is looking.

The garden, which is more of a yard with a small patch of scrubby grass, has been strung with lights. The bulbs hang from the trees like shining fruit.

Truth is, I didn't expect Norman to be here. Last time we spoke on the phone, his voice had an unfamiliar edge to it. I'd suggested we could still meet up, have the occasional cinema night, and he'd hit back with: 'Yes, I'm sure you'd like that, wouldn't you?' before cutting me off. Later, when we texted, he blamed his battery, but I reckon he'd switched off his phone, knowing it would hurt me not being able to check in on him. I'm wondering whether angry is better than sad. Angry says: *I'm moving on*. Sad is just … the opposite. I see him through the kitchen window now, helping himself to another can of beer, sloshing it into his glass. I take a deep breath in through my nose and let it out slowly, imagining the breath curling through the air and up, up towards the trees, up, up over the rooftops and away.

'Hey, Lou!' A packet of cigarettes wafts in front of my face and an elbow digs me in the ribs, prompting me to budge up. It's Bev.

I take a cigarette, even though I don't want one. Norman hates it when I smoke.

'That the guy you told me about?' says Bev.

'However did you guess?'

'From the fact that he talked about you for ten minutes straight. Jeez, Louise. The guy's obsessed. What the hell did you do to him?'

'He's a lovely guy but kind of… Let's just say it was *intense*.'

We'd only been together a couple of months when he

invited me to his parents' house for the weekend. 'You seem too nice to be a career girl.' Over Sunday lunch, his mother had looked at me with an almost hungry look in her eye. 'At your age, Louise, Norm was a toddler and his sister was on the way. We grew up so quickly, didn't we, Phil?'

Norman's father gave a weary smile. 'Excuse my wife,' he said, and then he whispered to me, so everyone could hear: 'Run, run away, while you still can!' Norman and his mother cracked up, and I did too.

Later, when she showed us to our room, she made a point of telling us that the beds could be pushed together, that she was sorry about the Spiderman bedding and the lack of curtains. 'We never got around to it,' she said. 'But it's quite private up here in the attic, and starry skies are restful, I always think.' Perhaps that was the night when I first felt the sickness, although I might be conflating the two. It was the first time that everything felt as if it was on the wrong track, and rapidly accelerating.

That same night, as we lay in the baking heat of the attic room on those single divans, Norman rolled towards me and cupped my face with his hand. 'Louise, they *love* you,' he said, 'and I do, too.'

'I know.' The words I didn't say hung there a while, and Norman rolled onto his back, his face glowing a dusky blue.

'It's okay, if you don't,' he said, finally.

But it wasn't that. Everything had changed, I just didn't know it.

A week or two later, I slipped out in my lunch break to buy a pregnancy test. I'd been getting migraines, accompanied by an unshakeable fatigue. When Norman tried to kiss me, I hugged him tightly. 'Please,' I said to him, 'please slow down.'

That day in the office toilets the blue cross for positive was unmistakeable, but I bought two more on the way home, just in case it had been wrong. We had been careful, hadn't we? I imagined his mother, patting my blooming middle as if it were an extension of herself.

'Lou,' said Bev, 'you're going to burn your fingers on that cigarette butt. Here—' She takes it from my hand and stamps it out on the patio. 'You didn't really want that, did you?'

'Sorry, I thought I did.' I had so wanted a moment of recklessness, but it's as if a switch has been flicked on, a sensible switch that makes me consider things like consequences.

'You've been miles away, Cleopatra,' Bev says. 'So far away, in fact, that your eyeliner is starting to run.' She bunches up the cuff of her silk Lady Diana blouse to wipe at my face. 'Seriously, Lou, that guy must be bad news.'

'I'm the bad news, more like.' I had no idea about Norman's mother. Strange, how the happiest people are sometimes the saddest underneath it all. When he told me things were difficult, that she would need a spell in hospital, I suppose it gave me another reason to say nothing about the baby. Or the baby that never would be. I had already booked a place at the clinic to discuss my options. It was better that way, I told myself. I would tell him just as soon as things were better.

'Speak of the devil,' she says, and I look up to see Norman walking towards us, holding his pint glass in front of him very, very carefully. 'I'll leave you to this *femme fatale*,' says Bev. 'These sausages don't look especially appetising now.' She prods them with her finger, then, with a sly grin, dumps them in the flower bed behind us and heads back to the kitchen with the empty tray.

'I would have eaten those,' says Norman.

'With your bandages?' I say, and he shrugs. I notice there's a gap in the bandages on his neck. His skin is flushed pink. 'Anyway, I've just remembered, aren't you supposed to be evil? Wasn't Claude, the guy who played you, part of my cinematic education?' Once upon a time Norm had tried to convert me to those old films.

'Not evil. Misunderstood.' He waves his pint glass at me. 'Want some beer?'

I raise my gin and tonic. The drink is just for show. I still don't feel up to it, though the sickness went away pretty quickly in the end. 'Cleopatra wasn't much of a beer drinker,' I say. 'Look, Norm, I'm glad you could make it. It's good to see you, looking so…'

'Invisible?' He laughs. 'I'd already bought the bandages.' I imagine it's a joke but it's hard to tell through the disguise. 'Did you know, Claude Rains had a speech impediment? He called himself *Wains*.'

'As in, *The Wain in Spain stays mainly on the Plain*?' I never made it to the appointment, after all. That was the morning the spotting began – a little at first, and then full-on cramps. And although I never wanted the baby, although it was a collection of cells – not a baby at all, I told myself – losing it was painful in every way. It felt careless, stupid, like I could have tried harder. And, really, I should have told Norman. I slip my fingers into my glass and take out an ice cube. I like to feel the crunch between my teeth, the numbness on my tongue.

'Exactly,' he says.

I open my mouth, trying to shape it into the words I need. 'Norm…' I put my hand on his arm, leave it there a moment.

He tilts his head as if he knows, but the words don't come. And then, thankfully, he rescues me: 'I'm not convinced

Cleopatra put whole ice cubes in her mouth,' he says. Norman has spent a lifetime avoiding difficult conversations, preferring not to know. And who else would tell him about this but me?

'I feel certain – if refrigeration had been a thing in Egypt – Cleopatra would've been a champion ice cruncher,' I reply. In the corner of the lounge, by the open patio door, Alice is holding a bowl of olives and looking in my direction. She makes a sign, like she's cutting off her own head, which would work if she were Anne Boleyn, but seeing as she's Beyoncé, it takes quite a leap of imagination.

'I can see you have places to be,' he says.

'It's just that I promised Alice I'd hand out the vol-au-vents. I never asked, how's your mum these days? Is she coping?'

Norman lowers his head. 'She's not,' he says, simply. 'It's slow progress. I haven't told her about us and she keeps asking and I...'

'These things aren't easy.'

'No. Being invisible doesn't exactly help matters.'

'I was being serious.'

'I know. But serious doesn't suit us, does it?'

'I guess not,' I say.

'Time to head home.' He turns to face the house, spilling beer on his shoes. 'Should probably lose the bandages, too. You made a great Cleopatra, by the way.' As he pushes through the crowd, people give him space. They whisper, wondering who he is. Perhaps it was wrong of me to finish things without explaining. But it would have been too much, the weight of it all.

When Norman waves through the patio door, I wave back. I can tell from the way he leans, hesitant to leave, that he is far from okay. But he will get better, I tell myself. And things could have been much, much worse.

Finally, it's come back to me, the scene from the film. We watched *The Invisible Man* at that old cinema he loves, the one that smells of velvet and tobacco, the one where they serve cups of tea in proper cups. Didn't the story end with Claude Rains, visible once again? As the lights went up, Norm turned to me. 'Wasn't his face sublime,' he whispered, 'even in lifelessness?'

I nodded in agreement and told him that even though an ending is sad, it can still be beautiful. *More* beautiful, I like to think.

EMILY DEVANE is a writer, editor and teacher from Ilkley, West Yorkshire. Her first print publication was the Bath Short Story Award Anthology 2015. She has since won the Bath Flash Fiction Award, a Word Factory Apprenticeship and a Northern Writers' Award. Her fiction has been nominated for Best Small Fictions (finalist), Best of the Net (finalist) and a Pushcart Prize, and features in *Best Microfictions 2021*. She recently won third prize in the *SmokeLong Quarterly* Grand Micro Contest and has work forthcoming in *Ambit*. Emily teaches creative writing workshops (@wordsmoor) and is a founding editor at *FlashBack Fiction*.

Acknowledgements

Each year, we've needed to expand our team as the Bath Short Story Award continues to grow. Ad Hoc Fiction handles our administration, which involves processing the entries, dealing with enquiries and publishing our anthology. This allows time for the core team and additional readers to select the stories. Each story is read by at least two readers who recommend their favourites for the longlist. Along with Alison Woodhouse, Jane Riekemann and Jude Higgins, our readers in 2021 were:

Audrey Anand
Claire Beazley
Rachel Clements
Catrina Davis
Zoe Duffy
Tracy Fells
Shelley Hastings
Michelle Hemstedt
Asha Krishna
Katie Oliver
Amanda Read
Georgie Young
Dylan Spicer

We thank them for their hard work, dedication and enthusiasm. As always, we're indebted to Elinor Nash whose original stunning collage has been adapted for each year's cover. Elinor won our 2014 award and her artwork can be seen on https://www.elenash.com/